QUE SERA SERA

whatever will be... will be

SOHRAB KHANDELWAL

Notion Press Media Pvt Ltd

No. 50, Chettiyar Agaram Main Road,
Vanagaram, Chennai, Tamil Nadu – 600 095

First Published by Notion Press 2021
Copyright © Sohrab Khandelwal 2021
All Rights Reserved.

ISBN 978-1-68523-316-7

This book has been published with all efforts taken to make the material error-free after the consent of the author. However, the author and the publisher do not assume and hereby disclaim any liability to any party for any loss, damage, or disruption caused by errors or omissions, whether such errors or omissions result from negligence, accident, or any other cause.

While every effort has been made to avoid any mistake or omission, this publication is being sold on the condition and understanding that neither the author nor the publishers or printers would be liable in any manner to any person by reason of any mistake or omission in this publication or for any action taken or omitted to be taken or advice rendered or accepted on the basis of this work. For any defect in printing or binding the publishers will be liable only to replace the defective copy by another copy of this work then available.

Blessed is the paper, blessed is the pen, blessed is the ink-pot and blessed is the ink.

Blessed is the writer, O Nanak, who writes the True Name of God.

— Guru Nanak

To my mama and papa…

To love, and the artist in everyone…

Acknowledgements

In 10th standard, I had for the first time shared with people that I wanna be an author. And at that time, most of my friends said you should be an actor, you are a far better actor. I did become an actor and with this book, I'm also an author now.

I want to start by thanking my mother, Dr. Kuljeet Kaur, for inculcating in me the habit of reading books very early in my childhood. It planted the seed in me of being a storyteller.

I want to thank my father, Gp Capt Ashwani Kumar, for believing in my writing and for continued support.

I thank my sister Dr. Nayantara for being my silent cheerleader throughout life.

I want to thank one of my best friends, Sanam Sekhon, perhaps the first person to encourage me to write my book. I was still working with Infosys when I had the idea of writing a book. There were some lonely times when I couldn't find a friend, but I always had you. I can't thank you enough, for standing by me, and for encouraging me to keep writing whatever I was undergoing in life.

I want to thank my uncle Charanjit Singh Jaura who has been like a life coach to me. Through some of the darkest moments in my life, you pushed me on to keep working, keep writing. I thank you most for always being a listener to me.

I want to thank Dr.Mandeep my friend and doctor. I was finally able to express myself freely and concentrate on my work.

Thank you Khodus Wadia. You have always been a mentor to me in not just voicing and acting but in storytelling. Your invaluable advice made it possible for me to create characters like Kabir and Lucia.

Thank you Aanand Mahendroo sir for being the institute you are and for having me as your student and for always appreciating and nurturing the writer in me.

Thank you Nithya Shanti, for being both a friend and mentor. Your advise on daily writings formed a crucial foundation for my writing routine later.

Thank you Neha Chandok for advising me to write whatever came to me first and in any order. It helped me cross the initial hesitation.

Thank you Sundeep Misra sir for your invaluable tips on how to write daily and form a routine. It was only because of that, that I could finish the book.

Thank you Ketan Bhagat for sharing your experience as an author and introducing me to my editor Indranil.

Thank you, Indranil Mukherjee for your comments and suggestions that made me push to make this book better.

Thank you, Alakh Niranjan, aka Jay, for your tips on self-publishing and encouragement to take the plunge with Notion Press.

Last but not least, I thank you, Nira Suarez my dearest friend for your belief in me and your unconditional support. Thank you for being my inspiration. You also went on to play beautifully the role of Lucia in the film - Que Sera Sera.

I also want to thank the Notion Press team especially Hema, my publishing manager for doing an excellent job with the cover and putting this book together.

It is the blessings of many people that I have been able to put this story together for you all to read. I might have not been able to take everyone's name but I thank you all for your continued love and support.

I give thanks to the muse and all those who have written before me.

Thank you Universe, Creation, Life, God for all the moments that led to this moment and for this moment that will lead to many more.

Thanks and God bless!

Peace, love n joy,

– Sohrab khandelwal

"Oh, the Places You'll Go"

– Dr. Seuss

"Go on. Do the divergent. Paddle upstream and surrender to unfamiliar tributaries"

– Nithya Shanti

One

"YEAH, MOST OF the luggage has been sent. I'm gonna pick the stuff later... Well, I'm just gonna spend the time in the city... yeah, yeah I'm okay... I don't know... No! The new tenant has to move in today... Yeah... So just gave the key and am now heading to the café... Thanks for everything... *Achaa*, I'm entering the lift... Will call you later..." Kabir disconnected the call as he entered the lift.

It was one of those old style lifts that had twin grill doors which had to be closed manually requiring some effort unlike the automatic ones but in exchange, it allowed the passengers a view of the outside. A lot of the older societies in Mumbai had such lifts. The phone call wouldn't have disconnected in the lift, but Kabir was feeling too emotional to carry on the conversation, not wishing to be probed further. He was leaving the flat to never come back again. So many wonderful memories was all that he had for luggage now and well, also a small knapsack that held a phone charger, a book, a notebook, a pen; all things required to help him through the day. The rest of his stuff, which was a guitar and a rucksack filled to the brim with books and clothes, was lying at his friend's place. He planned to pick it up the following day before heading to the train station. Two years had gone by so quickly, that's the most he could afford. His savings were all finished and now he had no choice but to head back to his old life. Somehow, he had managed to extend his tenure by a month by living frugally but Mumbai is expensive, and it couldn't go on for longer.

He had never even given it a thought that he might have to go back to his old job again. What was he going to say to them? With what confidence and panache he had left his old life, Kabir mused, as he turned the volume up to drown his thoughts. *John Mayer* was singing *Why Georgia Why* in his ears. Last day in Mumbai, the song was rather apt in helping him deal with the flood of emotions he was going through right then. Music somehow always helped in coming to terms with things, well, at least it did for Kabir. No matter what it was, break-ups, money troubles, family problems, failures, or even the death of a dream, he had a song for every occasion. And if he couldn't find the right song for the moment he would simply write that song. That's what he did, or that's what he loved to do. He wrote songs.

Kabir was a romantic at heart and music reverberated in his soul in all its shades. He was a poet like his famous namesake but not so much a saint like the enlightened one, who lived many years before him. This Kabir of today was still affected by the uncertainties of life. But one couldn't expect more from a 25-year old except to perhaps fight the world. That's exactly what Kabir had done. After all, to fight against your family's pressure to chase a dream and pursue your passion is as good as fighting the world. Very few have the courage to do that. Fewer still manage to succeed at it.

Kabir was a tall, languid guy with just the slight belly protruding that shows itself when you have not been eating right or sleeping well. He had a handsome looking suntanned face with a beard that was not many days old. He didn't care much for his looks or eating habits that made him look a couple of years older than he actually was. But his clear brown eyes reflected the innocence of a child that had remained untouched by the conditioning of society. Today, they reflected a dignified defeat in the face of circumstances. A warrior who had fought well but lost. But who are we to say what is defeat and what is triumph? Time has a funny way of changing the perspective, every now and then. Even though Kabir didn't have much money he was rich at heart. He always had all the time in the world, and that's one thing he liked to give himself and others even in a city where nobody could afford to give time to anybody.

The society watchman stood up promptly as he saw Kabir approaching, who handed him a couple of hundred bucks and a million dollar smile.

"Don't keep all the money for yourself, Bhogender! Share it with Panditji who will come for the night shift!" Kabir teased the watchman at the society gate in a Hindi dialect native to the watchman. His voice was warm, friendly, evoking a shy smile out of the chap. For most people he

was a rebel of sorts, for some like the watchman, just the happy-go-lucky guy, for a few others, a talent waiting to be recognized.

Very few people were party to what Kabir's inner thoughts were as he usually maintained a casually optimistic persona. Well, at least most of the time. When he couldn't keep his feelings inside any longer, it poured out in the form of music and poetry. Little riddles waiting to be understood and loved but that's what every person is. A riddle wanting to be understood and loved.

Kabir walked out the gate with the most casual long strides, never looking back.

Two

IT WAS STILL early in the morning when Lucia reached Mumbai. She felt a bit tired, but her dark brown eyes gave a hint that her soul was rejuvenated. A month of travelling through India can have that effect on anybody. She was ruing that she had to come back to Mumbai as a flood of memories came rushing to her. But that's how it was for now and there are somethings you just have to chug through. She had a flight to New Delhi at night. A few hours of waiting at the Delhi International Airport and then a flight at 11 in the morning to take her back to her home, Barcelona. There comes a time in every traveller's itinerary when they just want to snuggle into their beds because nothing else would suffice. And that moment had come for Lucia the moment she stepped out of the train on to the platform in Mumbai. She had had a good night's sleep on the train. But it didn't make sense getting a hotel room when she wouldn't be spending the night there. Adding to that was the fact that her expenses had already crossed the limits. Travelling in India might be cheap but there were always so many glittering things to buy and indulgence in this aspect had made her pockets lighter but her heart richer. So instead of spending the day indoors in a hotel, she thought she might just sit in a cafe, have her coffee first and then figure out from there. Being in Mumbai was not exactly how she had thought it would be as a whirlwind of thoughts were muddying her otherwise clear thinking. When she had first arrived in Mumbai at the beginning of her trip, she had a fairy tale in mind, but life has always a way of surprising when we least expect it. So while things took a complete 360-degree turn for her in Mumbai, it also led to a solo trip across India on a journey of self-discovery.

Lucia was an attractive 26-year old woman, about 5'7 tall, with light brown hair, and an athletic body. Stronger than she looked, she had been a ballet dancer and those who have danced know ballet is as strong as it gets. There was a certain grace in her movement which only lent her an air of royalty. This grace made many eyes turn as she floated along with her heavy rucksack into the cafe's outdoor sitting. She was casually dressed in her black leggings and a loose orange shirt hung over a tank top and sea blue suede leather sandals. A black metal intricately designed necklace bought in southern India adorned her long and slender neck. She hardly wore any make up, just a little eyeliner was enough to highlight her big, brown eyes. She was dressed for comfort without compromising on style. Her light brown hair flowed in the light morning breeze and metal bangles jingled in her arms while a *payal* tinkled languidly around her ankle. All of it had the effect of slowing down time for people around her. She hadn't taken note yet that time was malleable but then today was a day she would discover many things.

By now Lucia was quite used to the attention, which came with being a fair-skinned foreigner travelling in India. The attention that became ten-fold if you were a woman. But even though she had gotten used to the stares it didn't mean she liked it. She took a table next to a guy who seemed absorbed in a book and sipping on what could only be some variant of a cold coffee. That seemed like a safe bet. She wasn't in a mood to be bothered by anyone least of all by an Indian guy. So many had randomly come up to her so many times and tried to flirt with her that she was fed up with it. She had found it really difficult being alone in India. And right now she just wanted to spend one day without being bothered by anyone. The guy with the book looked at her, smiled faintly and went back to his reading. It was a smile of acknowledgement and nothing more. She gave a polite smile back, settled herself in the chair after plonking her rucksack down. The bag was heavy and oh, what a relief it was to get it off! All she was hoping now was that this cafe served a good coffee. That was another tricky part of being in India: finding good coffee wasn't always easy. A good chai you could get anywhere, but a good coffee, not so much.

She took out her book, as she looked around and got a feel of the place. It was only 9, and the winter sun in Mumbai was gentle and playful in the morning. So sitting outside was not a bad option. There wasn't much traffic either, so as of now, no honking on the streets too. It could get quite overwhelming for Lucia, this Indian traffic. And the sound of the horns was like this constant background noise that filled the air. It can get a while to get used to it. Well, actually you never get used to the honking, you simply get used to yourself being annoyed by it.

Three

KABIR NOTICED THIS attractive foreigner lady with her heavy rucksack taking a table next to his. It was an unusual sight demanding attention, and it drew an involuntary smile out of him. She was not your usual hippie tourist. No tie-and-dye kurtas , no Alladin pants, no dreadlocks, or extra piercings, just a heavy necklace around her neck which any woman could wear. Nothing except the rucksack to indicate that she was a tourist though, a lot of foreigners did live in Mumbai. But one quick look at her gave him pause. His concentration broke from the book that he was reading, "The Power of the Subconscious Mind" by Joseph Murphy.

When Kabir first noticed Lucia, a part of him wanted to initiate a conversation with her, but then better sense prevailed. This voice suggested that it would be rather forced and would make him come across as too eager, so he went back to his book. Joseph Murphy was somehow making a lot of sense to him today. He had had this book lying around on his shelf for a long time, but his hands always seemed to skip the mark whenever he had thought of reading.

Now even though Kabir went back to the book, a part of his brain continued to ruminate over her. And thoughts like—maybe he could talk to her later or was it fear that stopped him from striking up a conversation, and so on kept whirling in his mind until Joseph Murphy finally managed to bring his reluctant reader back to his pages. But it wouldn't be for long.

There was a time when Kabir used to find these self-help books funny, and he would often even berate them, make fun of them and the people who read them. And in his defence titles like *The Power of Thinking Without Thinking,* or *Rich Dad, Poor Dad* were almost asking for it. But lately he had been reading them voraciously. These books somehow made sense to him largely because they helped him forget being lonely. In that sense books are like people, they come into your life only at the opportune time.

Earlier Kabir had been drooping onto the table, immersed in his book. Perhaps that's how the expression "drowning in the books" arose. But now all of a sudden Kabir had gotten conscious of his posture and he sat upright. He even tidied up his otherwise unkempt hair by the most casual brush of hands, and even adjusted his long unbuttoned sleeves. He was wearing a broad brown leather arm band on his left forearm next to a rusty old chronograph that once belonged to his grandfather. The watch had a brown leather strap that went rather well with the armband. It made a style statement of coolness. Kabir made sure it was visible now as he sat with a straight back. He had, perhaps unconsciously, crossed one leg over the other, pointing it at Lucia. Nobody was noticing it. Perhaps there was nothing much to read in the position of the legs but ask an ardent student of body language and you were sure to be given some remarkable analysis.

Kabir sipped out of the pink straw of his takeaway cold coffee in the manliest way possible, reading the mysteries of the subconscious mind. Ironically, he was quite unaware of its movement in him.

And even before his grandfather's watch got a chance to prove it's functioning, he was back to his old posture, drowning in the book, his hair back to their tousled state. But the watch would get its chance to show its worth later in the day, when keeping track of time would be of utmost importance. And the human mind would not be a reliable instrument to do so.

Four

LUCIA ORDERED HERSELF a café au lait, and she read her *Sartre* to take her mind off the happenings that took place a month back in Mumbai. She had much preferred drifting in the Indian countryside or just travelling by train and staring out the window watching the endless landscape changing hues. An interesting observation she had made was of the subtle change in the colours of sunset across the landscapes. It was altogether a healing experience watching the thoughts to arise, culminate and come to their natural end under the watchful gaze of an attentive mind. The city with its manifold distractions doesn't give one the same luxury. Thoughts arise in plenty but then they let loose like children in a kindergarten without adult supervision. Books in such a scenario can help in a way not entirely different from a nanny or a babysitter.

She had been dreading coming back to Mumbai but today, coming back after a month, it didn't seem as bad as she had thought it would be. A shy waiter brought her the coffee, it smelled good. And there was brown sugar. What more do you need to make a morning better, thought Lucia, as she kept the book aside and added a sachet of sugar quite meticulously. It was her observation that there were always two types of guys she encountered in India. There were those who were too confident and smooth talkers or there were the ones who were too shy to talk and would even avoid making much eye contact with her, like the waiter who had just served her coffee. The irony was that she preferred to talk to those who were too shy to converse. The thought was amusing to her, and the coffee smelled good, and it passed her taste test. With that first sip, it felt now that passing the next few hours in the city wouldn't be too hard. What's more, she had almost forgotten about her ex and the apprehensions of running into him. As some of the tension released, her back straightened and her body eased into poise. Even in the way she sat and read a book there was grace. When people can't understand as to why they find someone attractive, most of the times it can be attributed to a good posture. In Lucia this often overlooked trait was accentuated, and few could have resisted looking at her just once.

Five

SHE NOTICED THE guy sitting at the adjoining table, absorbed in his book and made a mental note to herself – the shy type. He was wearing a lumberjack checked shirt, mustard-blue in colour. And his hair seemed a bit untidy. He sat with his chin resting on his fist on the table, absorbed in the book like only children can be. The guy looked very relaxed, quite unfazed by the surroundings. On a different day she might have fancied sketching him but not today. She again got back to her reading. *Sartre* always made sense to her. Sartre said "the other is hell". A guy came up to her just then as if on cue.

"Excuse me, can I join you?" asked the chappie, as he approached Lucia's table from the side taking her by surprise. He was wearing a US Polo shirt, the sort that's popular with people who have never been to a polo field. The collars were upturned to advertise the word *cool* emblazoned there, and leaving nothing to chance, he sported big-framed sunglasses. Blue denims and untied ankle-high sneakers completed his oh-I'm-so-cool look.

"No," Lucia said politely after a quick but careful glance at the source of this unpalatable intervention between her and *Sartre*. But an oblivious Mr Polo persisted and removed his sunglasses to make eye contact and leaned forward, making Lucia lean a little back. Mr Polo was not the brightest student of the subject of Body Language.

"Okay, let's do one thing, maybe we should go somewhere else to get to know each other better?" Mr Polo was ill at ease with English, but his mannerisms were a confident homage to what the popular culture terms as a fuck-boy.

Wow! This guy has got some balls, Lucia thought as she replied curtly, not a bit amused.

"No, I'm okay here. Please don't disturb me."

"Why don't you give me your WhatsApp number? We can talk later!" Mr Polo was not to give up easy, keeping up the smooth act.

"No, man. I'm reading my book, can you please leave me alone? Okay?" said Lucia with irritation now.

It has been researched it takes three times for an average mind to register something new. He backed down and Lucia once again went back to her book. Where was she now she wondered, her eyes darting between sentences. But before she could get her mental cursor back into the text, something happened that came as a complete surprise, leaving her fuming and flabbergasted and proving in essence that Mr Polo didn't possess an average mind.

"Okay one selfie!" Mr Polo swooped in from behind, knelt down beside her, and out came his phone camera, ready to take a selfie. The perfect camera angle for a good selfie requires practice. Mr Polo had spent enough time to know that with his arm stretched up, his face had to be right beside Lucia for the perfect shot.

The concept of personal space and privacy eludes most people as much as rocket science. And swear words have from time immemorial served the purpose of connecting people with their native tongue.

"HEYY! What are you doing! ¡*Los puta!* ¡joder!" Lucia's first instinct was to cover her face with one hand, palm facing out and the next was to abuse in her native language.

"Okay, cool, relax!" Mr Polo mumbled, visibly embarrassed with all the stares that he got from everyone around. Still blissfully unaware of the concept of personal space, he slunk away thinking today was not his day. The selfie too turned out to be a blur.

Meanwhile Lucia was left flustered as anybody would have been in her place.

Six

ANOTHER THING ABOUT swear words is that no matter what language they are in, they are sure to attract everyone's attention including Kabir's. Although he had been privy to the conversation and had even glanced once or twice, it hadn't evoked much interest in him figuring the lady had it in control. Plus such things happened in India dime a dozen. But now he sat upright, distracted from his book, taking a closer look.

The first thing he noticed was the strain in Lucia's eyebrows. There was a stark change in his neighbour's mood who looked visibly upset. He felt sorry for her but what could he do so he just went back to his book. That's just how it was in India, women had to endure a lot of inconveniences of such sort. Kabir had seen a lot of this nuisance growing up and being the sensitive person he was, he had even written a song about it that had gained quite a bit of popularity in his college days. But he couldn't concentrate now thinking about the woman next to him.

The following chain of thoughts in the form of a dramatic inner monologue preceded Kabir's impulse to strike up a conversation with Lucia.

The poor woman was enjoying her coffee and had seemed rather happy but now she's all upset. It takes a second to spoil someone's mood. How unfair is that? And it was a bad example being set up about India by jerks like these. He asked himself why don't people understand this? Of course one can approach a woman and ask her out but not by infringing on the privacy and start taking photos and stuff. And now she would tell this incident to ten other people. But there wasn't much that could be done or is there...

"Excuse me, are you a celebrity?" asked Kabir with schoolboy sincerity, looking up from his book, surprising himself as much as Lucia with the spontaneity.

"What?" retorted Lucia who was still upset, hoping instinctively it wasn't another unwanted admirer.

"Are you someone famous?"

"What! Why?" Lucia was a bit confused now.

"No, I mean this is the third guy who has tried to take selfie with you?" Kabir spoke with glint of smile in his eyes but with a rather serious tone.

"Well, it's been happening ever since I came to your country... you know!" Lucia got the joke. Okay the guy is funny she thought. But she was upset and in no mood to talk to anybody. Her guard was up.

"I'm sorry, but we are just too fascinated with white skin." Kabir was sincerely apologetic, and it reflected in his tone having a rather disarming effect on Lucia. He understood it is only when people can't understand the 'Why' that they tend to remain angry.

Its these unanswered 'whys' that upset people so much. And they feel better when an explanation for that 'Why' is given. If they are able to see the truth in that explanation, then nothing like it.

"Yeah, tell me about it!" Lucia said with a big sigh and went back to her book. She felt a bit better now because what the guy had said made sense but what didn't make sense was why they are fascinated with white skin? What's their problem? Another why had come instead of the first one now. She didn't know that most Indians are still living with a colonized mind. Her mind tugging on new whys making it hard to concentrate on the book and the mental cursor was all over the place.

"You know, I'm really sorry... on behalf of all those people who tried to intrude into your space." Kabir was succumbing to impulses that made him say the right words at the right moment.

"No, you don't have to be," said Lucia, quite surprised by this gesture from a complete stranger. She did feel better at being treated like a real person and with due respect.

"No, but I really am."

Lucia took a moment to study this person, she was bemused and also a bit curious. The guy was sweet enough to make her feel better. A faint smile finally escaped her heart as would anybody's when they encounter someone earnest. Perhaps because you rarely encounter that these days. And just like that all the unanswered 'Whys' didn't matter anymore.

"Are you always like this?" she asked with a smile.

"Only on Mondays, Wednesdays, and Fridays," Kabir replied deliberately as if absorbed in some deep thought and grinned at his own remark. He really knew how to smile, and it was a melting and an infectious one. A smile that came straight from the heart, shone in the eyes, and could pierce through stone itself.

Lucia was no stone, she was just a person who had been hurt. How could she not smile along.

"So today is your day!" Lucia went back to her book. She was back with herself, and the mental cursor was back with the text to exactly where it had left off.

Seven

A COUPLE OF seconds passed between them in silence, perhaps it was a couple of minutes. It's well established that Time is relative, more so in the matters of heart. This was a matter of heart. Kabir saw the conversation coming to an end or so he thought. But unseen forces had taken over the command as they usually do when the intent is good, encouraging new thoughts in him. Shouldn't he at least introduce himself first. He was not going to let this conversation die. He can't let this conversation die. He has to speak to her. She doesn't even know my name.

"Hi, I'm Kabir." He thought of extending his hand but then the distance between two tables was too much. And would have made it awkward.

"Hi, I'm Lucia." Lucia replied without her previous hesitation. Similar unseen forces were nudging Lucia's boat forward into unknown waters.

"Lucia, nice to meet you!"

"Nice to meet you, too!"

"So where are you from?"

"Spain."

"Ohh! Hola, como estas?"

"Bien, y tu? You know Spanish?"

"I don't know what you just said there, I know those two-three words only!" laughed Kabir.

"Good try, though..." Lucia felt elated. Finding someone to talk to in your own language is a feeling almost like coming home.

"So where in Spain are you from?"

"From Barcelona."

"It's supposed to be a very modern city, isn't it?"

"Yeah.. So, hey, congratulations! You are not going to say Leo Messi, right?" exclaimed Lucia, surprised he hadn't mentioned the football club like every other Indian had done till now.

Kabir's chain of thoughts went in an overdrive. How dumb to not mention the football club! Of course the Barcelona football club, now why didn't I think of that. Moreover, he loved that club. He loved it ever since Figo had played for them and now Messi was his favourite. But wait! Did she just say congratulations? Why did she say congratulations? Was it sarcasm? These thoughts rushed through his head in a heartbeat. It was enough time for him to interject

"Oh yeah, actually Barcelona is my fav club and Messi is the best. There is nobody better than him!" said Kabir emphatically, making up for not saying it before though still wondering why she said congratulations.

"Oh yeah, everyone talks about football, but to tell you the truth, I'm not so much into it."

"Okay..." So that's why she had said congratulations, he thought.

At this juncture all of Kabir's thinking prowess was busy assimilating previously obtained information that he could use to continue the conversation. If someone were to have a glimpse of the workings inside his head they would have been impressed and perhaps even recommended it to be considered as a case study in various disciplines taught in a B school.

Now what was the name of that cathedral and who was that architect, he kept thinking hard and the name kept eluding him. It was not so hard remembering the name as it was enunciating it correctly. And enunciation is the name of the game or so he thought momentarily.

"Hey, so has that finished, how do you say his name... Gawdi, Goudi?"

"*Gaudi*? You know *Gaudi!*" Lucia exclaimed, pleasantly surprised.

"Yeah, that big cathedral... Sagra da..."

"*Sagrada Familia?* You know *Sagrada Familia!*" Lucia spoke in her pronounced Spanish accent, surprise in every syllable.

And at this point she shifted her body a little in her chair at an angle towards Kabir. And a student of body language would have said, she was now enjoying this conversation. She liked talking about Barcelona and not many people she had met talked about her city in terms other than football.

"Yeah, has that finished yet?"

"How do you know that? No, not yet. No, it's not done. No... I think Gaudi just designed it to keep people busy after his death. Like, you people go on working. I'm going, but you keep working. I will be watching you from the heavens." Lucia laughed at her own joke. She had often thought this but had never really voiced it until today. It was an impressive and beautiful structure but the whole idea of putting people to task really seemed funny as well. And what were the odds of a guy asking about Gaudi of all things in Mumbai?

She was making witty jokes so she's not just a pretty face. Kabir's endless thoughts were like a background music that kept with his mood or influenced it at times. He felt good. He was on the right track and a beaming smile wreathed his face.

Eight

"WHAT ELSE DO you know about Spain?" asked Lucia. She spoke fast, but that was merely because she was Spanish, and they do tend to speak fast. It has to do with how Spanish is syllable-timed language unlike English which is stress-timed language.

"I know Pablo Picasso, Dali, you know..." said Kabir quite casually as he thought about the paintings he had seen. He loved to watch paintings as they always inspired him to write. And the abstract and the surrealist had captured his imagination in a way like no other. The more abstract and surreal they were, the better they were at triggering his imagination. The limitlessness of thought in those paintings helped him break the monotony of rationale.

He would often spend time looking at paintings even on the Internet, although it was not quite the same thing. But economics had prevented him from making as many trips to Europe as he would have liked.

"You know the Spanish masters!" Lucia was pleased to hear someone talking of Spanish painters.

"Yeah, I do. So are you like Catalan or Espanyol, Espana, Spanish?" Kabir was confused with the correct term to be used.

"You know, you are the first person asking me that in India," remarked Lucia, grinning and mightily amused. This conversation had completely changed her mood and she felt much happier. If it takes a moment to lose your cool, it also takes just a moment to get the spring back in your spirits too.

"Really?" Kabir jumped albeit pleasantly. To Kabir it sounded quite normal; why would anybody not talk about that, he wondered, feeling better about himself. And congratulations spread among all the faculties inside him. The different departments that had been earlier busily tending to supply material for conversations stood up high-fiving. Not too different from how a space agency might feel at a successful launch.

"Yeah, I'm the first in my family to be brought up in Catalonia but I'm Spanish." Lucia said. She liked this guy's vibe. He was relaxed and wasn't trying to be someone or prove something. Lucia liked people who were natural. And she felt like knowing more about him. It could be also noted for those interested in the science of body language that Lucia had positioned herself facing Kabir now. The tensions of the previous encounter which had earlier made her stiff and distressed had dissipated leaving room for flow and poise to enter.

Nine

"SO KABER, KABIR?" Lucia fumbled with the pronunciation of the name. It wasn't that complex, she had come across much harder names, involving sounds that had been so new to her that her brain had felt little soundgasms.

"Yeah, Kabir... Kabir was like... a... a saint, a... a... a poet, you can find his wonderful writings, in English translation as well."

Kabir was fond of his name because he loved the writings of the great master and felt excited to speak about him. Yet he spoke deliberately with breaks and certainly not because he was hesitant. Whenever Kabir spoke with foreigners, naturally he felt he had to explain more because they didn't know his culture. So he relied on hand gestures and spoke well-chewed words. But he also felt as if he had all the time in the world and could express freely. It was partly because he didn't feel judged by them and partly because the listener too was making an effort to listen rather than just wait for their turn to speak. The result was that Kabir came across just as profound as he actually was.

"So Kabir the poet... where are you from?" Lucia's tone, coupled with being addressed as a poet, caught him off guard, making him blush. He was not used to being called a poet and nobody had called him as 'Kabir the poet'. It struck a chord inside that would echo for a long time.

"Ahh, thank you." Kabir muttered sheepishly under his breath as he gathered himself to explain where he was from while Lucia enjoyed the effects of her cafe au lait.

Unlike an American who often takes it for granted that that you have heard of places in their country most Indians tend to assume a more modest expectation while speaking to foreigners. Kabir was no different in this.

"I'm.. I'm from the north... Do you know a place called Punjab?" asked Kabir, unsure if she had heard of it.

"So you are the Bhangra people," smiled Lucia while her arms went up and did that popular Bhangra step involving the shaking of shoulders. Her twinkling eyes saying Kabir wasn't the only one who could impress with information.

"Yes! Yes, we are the Bhangra people!" Kabir pounded the table with a triumphant fist as a sudden surge of enthusiasm overtook him, his voice a few decibels louder, inviting a couple of stares from around the cafeteria. But he didn't notice any of that, his eyes were all for Lucia. Kabir's legs were dancing, his thumbs were twiddling, and his neck was nodding like Noddy, all in congruence with a nervous excitement. It was life in him that was vibrating with happiness.

"So... I see the big bag, where you headed?"

"Oh, nowhere but home! I just have my flight in the evening."

"Okay. So what plans for the day?"

"Nothing, just coffee, reading..." Lucia spoke a lot with her hands and her movements were rhythmic. She pointed to the coffee, her book and shrugged her shoulders; it could have easily come across as a dance step to someone who couldn't hear what the conversation was about.

"So what are you reading?"

Lucia lifted the book up, Kabir craned his neck to see the book. His movements could be a bit clumsy, but his voice was not. The little recognition had removed his inhibitions and he shifted gears from tenor to baritone.

"Jean Paul Sartre! Are you a feminist?" Kabir mimicked the tone of an animated news reader.

"Everyone should be!" she quipped, laughing at Kabir's antics. Lucia was not expecting to be asked such questions. She liked having an intellectual conversation and Kabir seemed to be offering that and was also funny. Not exactly the shy guy she had thought him to be earlier, but neither was he the smooth talker.

"Who isn't, right? Who isn't..." Kabir was grinning. Lucia was not just a pretty face but was smart and he just couldn't stop himself from talking to her. A strong, overwhelming desire to spend more time Lucia swept over him. Joseph Murphy would have to seek his reader's attention some other time after all.

Ten

AS THE LENGTH of their conversation grew, the duration of eye contact between them also grew. A sign of trust and companionship. Just as a comfortable silence was playing in the background even when the words paused. Like the silence written on sheet music, which becomes part of the music. Preconceived thought had ceased to exist in this conversation, they were simply flowing now.

"Hey! So, did you have breakfast yet?" Kabir asked in the hope that they could have breakfast together perhaps.

"No, not yet. I was just thinking of having a sandwich here." Lucia said as she glanced over the menu to decide on what she would eat now.

"No, no, no... You can't have breakfast here... The sandwiches are not good enough here!"

"No?"

"No, definitely not, you gotta have an authentic Mumbai breakfast," said Kabir emphatically.

"I don't know..."

"But I know. A place right around the corner," said Kabir quite sincerely.

"I don't know..." said Lucia with a faint smile.

"Oh yeah, you will love it!"

The rudiments of making any new decision involve a tug of war between two opposing views. It starts with one thought pitted against the other and soon enough there are other thoughts joining either side from different angles. Most of the times it's a futile exercise as the decision has been made much before but an ostentatious performance is an act to assuage the nerves. The first of Lucia's internal tug of war for the day began with – she could go have breakfast with him, he seemed like a nice fun guy. But she was not in her city, could she really trust him. How far is the place? The bag is so heavy... I would have to carry it. But an authentic breakfast sounded better than sandwiches. Who knows it might be tasty. But it's too much effort...

"But I just met you..." Lucia's words were half-hearted and her protest weak. While the tug of war continued within, delicately balanced, just a little nudge could decide the duel.

"Well, you can pay the bill... If you like..." said Kabir breaking into a laugh.

"Okay... fine," said Lucia with a smile, thinking yes, that's right, that's what I was worried about. Who is paying the bill? She would reflect on this conversation many days later and find it funny how that one sentence had helped make up her mind. What she didn't know was that an out of the box remark had simply put an end to the tug of war in her head, much like how a sudden downpour rain makes people forget what they were doing and simply make a dash for it.

Kabir called for the bill and as a true Indian offered to pay for her coffee too, but she wouldn't allow. Neither was Kabir too pushy, like many Indians tend to become. He was familiar with the western culture where each paid for what they ate. With the bill paid off Lucia lifted the heavy backpack and tied the belt around her waist. And Kabir quickly slurped through the last drops of his cold coffee.

Eleven

MUMBAI IS A tropical coastal city but living here you tend to forget that fact most of the time. Largely because of it being a huge metropolitan city and a financial hub which makes it come across as a city of work rather than a place of quietude and calm that resonates with a tropical coastal side. Adding to that Mumbai has its fair share of skyscrapers. But there amongst all this hustle-bustle of Mumbai you can also find quaint colourful cottages with thatched roofs, ringed by the lazy coconut and palm trees. And here in these lanes with vividly decorated walls drawn over by anonymous graffiti artists taking inspiration from pop art, Bollywood classics, celebrities, and even comic book heroes, one forgets all the concrete, glass, traffic, pollution, and a growing population that is bigger than the population of some countries. Other than being on the beach it is here in such alleys that one feels the beat of a coastal city.

Kabir took the weight off Lucia's shoulders with his zealous tales about the city and India as they walked through these beautiful graffiti-filled lanes. Having travelled the length and breadth of India he was well versed with history. He had a treasure trove of trivia to share which he peppered with humour that Lucia listened to intently and couldn't help feeling that Kabir could make a good guide. She liked how he was proud of his country but at the same time affected by the prevalent poverty. She had some curiosity questions to ask about the various rituals and practices that she found too inexplicable and in all her time had never bothered to ask anyone before. Like why there was green chillies and lemon hanging everywhere. Kabir explained how it was to ward off the evil spirits and then joked that evil spirits are those spirits who when life threw lemons at them didn't make lemonade.

She had read a lot about India too but for now was content with listening. Better not to reveal all your cards at once, she thought to herself. Meanwhile her bag like all things heavy was beginning to get heavier with time.

Every now and then, Kabir would offer to carry the bag for her, and Lucia would politely refuse. They must have walked for half a kilometre or more by then.

"Kabir, how far is it? I don't wanna walk any more..." said Lucia, her attention to their conversation decreasing with every step.

"Why don't you let me carry it?"

"No, no, it's okay, I'm alright. Just tell me how far?"

"No, please let me carry it. Okay I'm too chivalrous to let you carry it any further!" He smiled cockily.

"Are you sure?" Lucia's eyes announcing *there is no coming back from it once you agree.*

"Of course." Kabir spoke confidently. But he had no idea how heavy the bag was.

Lucia removed the bag with feline grace. From there it took a couple of minutes for Kabir to strap the backpack on, it was too complex for his clumsy arms. There were way too many straps and he eventually got stuck in one of them.

"Wait, I'm stuck!"

Lucia, who had walked on, had to come back to disentangle him. The onlookers got a new sight of a foreigner helping an Indian disentangle himself from a bag. A student of philosophy would have found this a funny allegory. There was delay in the proceedings as Lucia couldn't control her laughter at the whole situation. Kabir's surprising clumsiness was rather endearing for her.

"Aah... Its ah... Not as heavy... As I thought...," gasped Kabir adjusting the straps by heaving the bag with a jerk.

At the end of it Kabir was left panting, less by the weight of the bag and more by the pressure of looking cool. Lucia helped tie the waist strap while Kabir stood still, an obedient schoolboy being dressed and combed for school.

"Wasn't it easier if I were carrying it?" Lucia asked coyly, her eyes betraying how amused she still was with the whole episode.

She held his Quechua knapsack in her arms besides a small, white ladies bag of her own. The sort that could be worn on your back. It qualified as a little knapsack in the way it was made but its aesthetics were of a handbag. This one more so, as it had a transparent heart shape in the centre, which gave a sneak-peek into the contents. There was a book, a notebook, and headphones that hid behind them the many secrets that a woman's handbag usually holds.

"Were you afraid that I was gonna run off with it?" Kabir joked now that he had got his breath back, adjusting his pride to the weight of the backpack which was making him bend slightly forward.

"I don't think you can run with that!" Lucia quipped.

She usually wore the persona of a dignified lady—which she was undeniably—but her playful nature would find a way to shine through her eyes especially in moments like these. Her eyes had the quality of not just highlighting what was being said but also conveying things that were often left unsaid, only to be sensed.

Twelve

THERE WAS MORE walking to be done and the bag couldn't dam Kabir's enthusiasm for the talking. He talked with this constant need to entertain people around him and more so when he was a bit anxious. He had grown a people-pleasing nature since childhood which worked quite contrary to his talents that required him to focus on himself. Perhaps that was the reason he studied engineering and even took up a job even though he had no inclination for it. An aptitude for doing something is often mistaken by most people as an attitude for doing it. It was certainly mistaken by his elders who thought Kabir's good score in maths meant that he should study engineering.

On the plus side, Kabir's nature made other people feel important.

Lucia found herself looking at the city in a new light. Most of her stay in India until now had been limited to the old towns and the other popular tourist destinations. She never really had paid much attention to urban India. It's always a different experience when you walk through a city. It leads to truly knowing the place and making it your own.

Quite like how a mountaineer summits a peak, the traveller too has to walk to make the city their own.

She felt Mumbai was at times like watching modern people put in an old timeline and sometimes people of past era put in a modern timeline.

"So what's the story of this backpack? Kabir asked. His gait was slower than before but not his gabbing.

"What do you mean, 'story'?" Lucia asked. The traffic had increased, and she was more alert. She had been on alert mode ever since she had first stepped out of the airport landing in India, but there exists a superlative of alertness which Lucia had discovered only when she had set foot in midst of traffic in India.

"Well, every backpack has a story. Where all they have been, how did you get to buy them and so on and so forth."

"Well this bag was gifted to me by my mom when I turned 18."

"Naice!" Stretching the first syllable of any word and extending it into a smile to describe something was Kabir's way of expressing how much it resonated with him.

"Yeah, she really encouraged me to travel."

"So where all have you travelled?"

"Peru, Amsterdam, Greece, Czech, Paris, now India…" Lucia's eyes were scanning everything. The different lines that made the space and the varied colours that filled it. As a painter Lucia loved the different visuals India offered her.

The pesky two wheelers, the cluster of ladies in their colourful sarees marching, suddenly stopping and then marching again and then stopping again like flamingos dancing, young girls in miniskirts scootering, talking incessantly on their earphones, bikers with the helmets in their arms to not spoil their hair, turning their heads only for women, the old man sitting in the courtyard with his newspaper and driving off flies, the loud, out of tune hawkers relentlessly calling out their wares, competing with the crows, and the old lady drying her hair with her head bent down, the auto-rickshaw buzzing frantically pausing near every pedestrian like bumblebee to a flower, and the swanky cars with their tinted windows, oblivious of the rest.

Did the word amalgamation form here in India? Lucia toyed with that thought while she described the places she had visited to Kabir. And she unconsciously compared them to her experience in India thinking how India had a bit of everything and yet India was like no other.

Kabir was on a different trip, nodding his head thinking how different her lifestyle was compared to his. The romantic in him needed little help to take off and as Lucia narrated her travel adventures, he imagined himself as an 18-year old traveling to the far off Machu Pichu or to the pyramids in Egypt which he had only seen on television.

Imagination is the saviour of those who haven't had the experience.

Thirteen

"WOW, I LOVE that thing about you *firangs*. I mean about foreigners, I mean, you know what I mean, you guys love to travel, and YOU TRAVEL. I so envy that!" Kabir said forcefully. Firang was a common slang in India for any Caucasian. Initially it was for the British but now it was used for everyone who was white.

"Not so much here?" It was hard for Lucia to not be amused.

Kabir shook his head as his life frayed itself for a moment in front of his eyes. He had always wanted to travel and do all the awesome things people his age group post about on social media. But here he was struggling to make ends meet by doing what he loved to do the most. Reminded of all the social media posts, people traveling to exotic places and celebrating life just made him aware of a void. It made him look down. He didn't yet understand that what he was doing was a brave thing to do. All of his little cells felt a mongrel complex. Just as his insides were about to play a melancholy tune, he noticed how his steps and Lucia's steps were in sync and that made him smile again.

"Well, you guys travel with bags, we travel with suitcases... Because you guys travel to travel, and we travel to immigrate!" Kabir laughed out loud. They say the people with the greatest sorrows laugh the loudest. If that were true then Kabir could be a living proof. It was almost like a defence mechanism of his to shoo away the unsettling melancholy. For the unaccustomed his laugh could be mildly shocking. But the positivity in it made up for lost ground making his listener invariably laugh along.

Lucia laughed thinking of all the subcontinent migrants in Barcelona. And now there were a few who had made it into her circle too.

"Hahaha... Yeah, oh my God... but it's true. There are a lot of Indians and Pakistanis..." Lucia stopped midway in sentence as it struck her immediately that she probably shouldn't have said it. She knew there's an animosity between the two countries, but she couldn't understand the reasons because they were both one country at some point. And she knew that both Indians and Pakistanis didn't like to be talked of in the same sentence, even though one can easily pass off as the other. They looked the same to her.

Kabir, oblivious to the inner workings of Lucia, looked at her enquiringly, wondering why she had stopped in the middle of the sentence. Meanwhile Lucia thought she had offended him in some way even more so because of the way he was looking at her. So they both just looked at each other suspended in thought like two characters from some

Alfred Hitchcock movie unaware of anything. Before long transforming them into Woody Allen's apologetic meta characters who give explanation about everything.

"I'm sorry I didn't, I shouldn't, have said it!"

"What!" It took a moment for Kabir to realize what she was referring to. And her concern amused him.

"No, it's okay. In fact, you know when I was in Madrid. I met this guy, and he was talking in Hindi with me. So I got really excited, you know... to find another Indian guy in a different country. That India-*wali* feeling, so I asked him 'where are you from in India?' And he replied, 'I'm almost Indian!' I was like what's 'almost Indian'? And he told me that he was from Lahore..." Kabir spoke animatedly, his hands flying left-right-centre. It was just entertaining to listen to him tell a story. He looked at Lucia who was listening intently, realising from her expression that she perhaps didn't know where Lahore was.

"Lahore is in Pakistan. Right? So I was like if this guy who is from Pakistan can say he is almost Indian then there is basically no difference in people. They want the same things, it's just the people in power who make a fool out of the masses and divide them."

For a bit they observed silence impenetrable by noises outside. Perhaps the silence was a mark of respect to the many who had succumbed to the violence of lines drawn on a map by a few. Or maybe it was just one of those spaces on tape that separates two tracks. Nevertheless, it allowed them both to be who they were. The rhythmic breeze kept pace with their steps, allowing little beads of sweat to take life but whisking them off before they could leave the trail marks.

Kabir thought perhaps they were a few decades behind their European counterparts who had had their fill of wars and learnt their lessons. And most of Asia was still reeling under wilful malice, with clouds of malevolence hovering always in the near distance. How long before they understand this? Bob Dylan found his way into his head while the answers were blowing in the wind.

It came as a pleasant surprise to Lucia that Kabir had visited Madrid. She impulsively felt that he could understand her better, even felt a little closer to him because he had visited her country. It was that feeling of familiarity which lessens the distance between two people, like discovering a part of you in the other. However small it might be, it doesn't matter. Perhaps that's why people like finding out that you share similar interests. And most of all, she liked how he spoke out his views with conviction, free of animosity. The more she got to know him, the better she felt around him. She liked him though she didn't know this yet but was soon to find out.

"Hey, we are there!" Kabir announced with a beaming smile, leading the way to this old Irani cafe.

Fourteen

THE INTERIORS OF an Irani cafe are basic. There is little that changes about them over the years. From the menu to the furniture, everything remains the same. So much so that it can be argued that the main function of Irani cafes is to preserve time.

Lucia and Kabir entered one of the popular Irani cafes of Mumbai. A solemn bald man in his late fifties sat at the front counter by the entrance. He sat aloof, as if uncaring who was entering or exiting. But while he bore a disinterested look, he noticed them all. The only time he moved was when one of the waiters brought in the cash along with the bill, he would then open the drawer put the money in and give the change back. Next to him was posted a note – that read *no mobile charging*. It could seem to most that the person was bored but he was from the silent era where people could sit and do nothing. He gave a nod when Lucia and Kabir entered this time capsule. A place that would slow the time was just the sort of thing you need when you want to get to know a person.

Along the same line behind the owner sat a much younger man on a much lower desk, whose task was to generate the bills and when he was not doing that, which was hardly ever, he was busy looking at his phone. His movements were more than compensating for his employer's lack of it. Next to him was set a fridge that showed off all sorts of coloured cold drinks in it. Adjoining it rested an empty cooling cabinet that one often encounters at the confectionary shops. Though nobody knew why it was always empty.

Opposite this whole set up were laid out 12 square tables, each with four chairs around them. The wooden chairs had white cane interweaved making up for the seat and the splat that had lost any resemblance to the colour white long ago. Every table was covered with a green felt cloth with a glass pane on top. Underneath the glass on the table were inserted the menus that one could read, four on every table facing the chair, making the job easy for the waiters. There were a couple of boards that hung, one of them boasted of it as certified Grade 2 place.

The comings and goings made sure the place was neither too full nor empty. Some came just for a cup of tea or a light snack like the *bun-maska* but there were others who came to try the various meat savouries or for a king-size meal. A big old round wall clock was the only thing on the creamish wall that had paint peeling off in places. The eatery's atmosphere gave Lucia the feeling that Time had perhaps forgotten to visit here. It was an open place with no air conditioning. Kabir and Lucia took a table that was right under one of the ceiling fans that didn't seem as anxious as them.

"So basically nothing changes about these cafes. Like even this place is what, 70 years old?"

"Oh, wow!"

Kabir explained with gusto the history of the Parsis in India and their role in making what Mumbai is today. He took pride in their accomplishments as if they were his own community. That he could transcend socio-cultural barriers and feel connected with people who were from different backgrounds was one of the underrated qualities about Kabir. And although he was busy doing most of the talking, he could observe that Lucia was comfortable there and it reassured him inexplicably.

Fifteen

LUCIA TOOK A cursory glance at the place while listening to Kabir. It wasn't anything impressive, but it definitely looked old and that lent it a charm of simplicity. It was surprisingly airy with ample sunlight and a decent level of hygiene discernible all around. The high ceiling had old fans that hung low over some of the tables and moved at an easy pace, unlike the rest of Mumbai. The vibe was relaxing.

"There is a high possibility that this menu is 70 year old, too," Kabir said, tapping his knuckles on the table. The waiters here were quick and proactive catering to several customers that visited on a regular basis. They were always zipping around the tables, like Indian taxis on road, never following a straight line, never bumping into each other. But unlike the taxis, the waiters here maintained a certain level of quietude.

When they were not serving, the waiters stood scanning the tables from near the kitchen never shying to make eye contact with the customer. Kabir ordered for a bottle of water and before he could order next— Bam!

There was a bottle of cold water on the table. He asked for water at room temperature. Bam! There was another bottle alongside the previous one. Before he could ask to take the cold one back, Poof! The waiter was gone.

It was one of those places where if you take time to order different items, there is a high possibility that they could be back with the first item you ordered before you ordered the next one. And it would all look like magic. So in a way, these restaurants were the perfect getaway for the modern man and woman. A time capsule without delayed gratification.

Kabir ordered on behalf of Lucia as well, it came as a pleasant surprise to him that they both were kind of vegetarians. The kind that eats eggs, so 'eggetarians', if you could call them that. Kabir didn't know of many foreigners who were vegetarians. He took it as a sign.

"So Kabir, what do you do?" Lucia had been meaning to ask him for a while.

"Well I sing, and I write." Kabir pausing between words because he somehow felt unsure today. Now that he had decided to go back to his old job was he really a songwriter anymore?

"Oh, wow, will you sing for me?" Lucia asked with childlike enthusiasm, eyes shining.

"Oh, not here, not now, not today," Kabir replied, taken a little aback with the request, while his mind was still dealing with an existential angst: should he pursue his dream that had until now offered little success or to go back to his dreary job which is what everyone wanted of him?

Lucia's interest in Kabir had increased knowing he was an artist. She had a soft corner for the artistic soul. She felt the world could be a harsh place and it was even more for the artists. An artist always saw things that others couldn't. She looked into his eyes wanting to know all he had seen.

Kabir broke away from the eye contact, he was not ready to be read. The waiter standing near the kitchen thought Kabir was looking at him and gave a reassuring glance back, gesturing the food was on its way. The waiter in that effect was the proverbial Chekhov's Gun. He had made himself visible and now he would have a role to play.

"Okay, so tell me what you write."

"I like to believe they are poems, songs, stories..."

Kabir was looking away, his mind full of a zillion other thoughts in that moment, predominantly about the struggle he had had to endure to do what he wanted to in his life and the lack of validation for his talents.

Lucia for the first time saw Kabir, the vulnerable. It was there to be seen even if just for the briefest of the moments, a moment that was gone in the blink of an eye. Her interest rose in him gradually like a wave that swept him towards her. The pull of the feminine, as Lao Tse would have said, is a mystery. Kabir looked directly at Lucia's eyes and the wave in her entered him as a wave of optimism.

Sixteen

"DO YOU LIKE poetry?"

"I love poetry."

"Do you wanna hear a poem?"

"I'd love to hear a poem..."

"a little shuffle, a little scratch, a little smile, a little clearing of the throat,

a little shuffle, a little scratch, a little smile, a little glance of nervousness,

a little shuffle, a little scratch, a little smile, a little sigh of readiness..."

Lucia moved her chair and leaned forward cupping her chin in her hand with her elbow planted on the table. And the way she looked at Kabir with all her attention, made his mind go blank and he couldn't remember any of his poems in that moment. It's ironical that the reason we communicate is to get attention and since we are not used to getting it so when we do get it, it envelops the desire to communicate. And only spontaneity can exist in that moment.

There is no I, there is no other. So when Kabir began to recite it was he who spoke the words, but it was also he who was the listener. The words were simply flowing in the moment through him.

Seventeen

"OKAY THIS ONE is called —-
    An Ode to a Coffee Table
    There two lovers were..
    Hands interweaved around a coffee cup...
    They inhaled presence...
    bonding them in breath...
    Lips parted listening...
    what they spoke in silence...
    Time struck and they left...
    A little more rich...
    A little less poor...
    And the stain of the coffee cup...
    Is the proof of those two...
    Lovers lost in time..."

The words knitted together lofted by Kabir's voice rich in timbre took them both floating into a state of reverie, from which both didn't want to emerge. There comes a time in performances where the performer and the audience become one, this was that time. And a comfortable hush ensued which is perhaps one of the most blissful moments of life. Where the mind is absolute, the body breathes effortlessly, and the soul shines forth brightly. It's a curse humans live with that makes them break such a reverie because it is sometimes too much to take in. It didn't matter who replied and who asked in such a moment.

"Do you like it?"

"It's beautiful..."

"I just got inspired right now..."

"Oh, come on!" Lucia blushed. It was impressive if he had actually made it in the moment. Her hand couldn't help touching Kabir's shoulder. He became an artist for her from that moment onwards, and everything about him would make more sense.

"Yep. This coffee table was too inspiring..." Kabir tapped the table with his knuckles. He had a triumphant grin. His day had been made.

For a while they were ethereal, then they became part of the rest.

Eighteen

THEY WERE BOTH somewhere else, oblivious of the public around them, floating on the magic carpet knitted by their imagination. And they would have remained there had it not been for their waiter. Their entry and exits are timed to create the most dramatic effect. Almost as if they are pushed onto the stage by the director on cue. Like a genie he popped up between them, dexterously conjuring the various dishes one after the other on their table, quite accurately guessing who had ordered what. Waiters who have waited on tables long enough can tell a lot about the customer from just what they order.

While the waiter carefully manoeuvred the many dishes on the small table, Kabir began to explain them to Lucia like a captain announcing the flight's arrival before landing.

"This is *bun-maska,* basically dollops of butter put inside the bun and you dip it in the chai like that and have it..." Kabir took a big bite filling his mouth having followed his own instructions.

"Okay, but I can take a smaller bite, right?" Lucia was grinning at Kabir's expression.

He had ordered some cheese masala omelettes, potato cutlets, and chai. They smelled delicious, and Lucia was hungry.

She loved the Indian chai and this one tasted good. Kabir explained that it's because they prepare the black tea and then add hot milk when they serve, while most other places they boil the tea and milk together. The food was heavy but the explorers that they were, knew that it's always good to start a day with a full breakfast.

Nineteen

"I HAVE AN idea... but... wait... So what's your plan?" Kabir asked. He had only one thought in his mind, spending more time with Lucia.

"Nothing really. I have the flight in the evening to Delhi." Lucia replied, eating through her bread and omelette. It was spicy just like everything was in India. The green chillies, the red chillies, the black pepper, and some chilli sauce were kept on the table, just in case you wanted to compete with a dragon.

"Oh yeah, you are going to Delhi... So you meeting some friends there...?" Kabir tried his best to not come across as overly inquisitive. It's hard when your whole attention is fixed on a person.

"No, I'll just wait at the airport. And then take my flight to Barcelona." Lucia sensed his curiosity.

"Oh hey... have you seen much of Mumbai?"

"No, not really."

"So, why don't you spend the rest of the day exploring the city with me?" Kabir put those words out as nonchalantly as he could. He was hoping against hope she would say yes.

"I don't know..."

"Why not? It would be fun! And in fact do you know Delhi is not a safe city for women. I'd even propose you postpone the flight to Delhi. Go early morning tomorrow and then later on to Barcelona!" Kabir said jovially. But he did not mean it as a joke. He had nothing against Delhi but just wanted some more with time Lucia. Something like this had not happened ever before to him. Sure, Kabir spoke to people and loved to spend time with them. But there was something different about Lucia. He hadn't come across a woman like her. It was not just how she was, it was about how he felt in her presence. There was a desire to tell her everything and to know everything about her.

Twenty

THAT LUCIA WAS surprised at Kabir's proposal would be an understatement. The saner part of her exclaimed no, but inside her a voice also said yeah, let's do it! That voice didn't reach her conscious mind. Instead, she chose to concentrate on the other voice that insisted she was perplexed. But the longer she dwelt on that, the louder the other voice was becoming. The capricious ways of universe had started the tug of war and this one was not going to be affected by rain or hail. He can't be serious, can he? Is he serious, he seems really serious, but no way I'm gonna delay my flight! Having breakfast is one thing but spending the whole day with a stranger! Finally a victor was declared albeit unconvincingly.

"I'm not sure if that's the best idea…" Clearly, she was still thinking aloud.

"Yeah, I don't know if it's the best, but it would be a good one…" Kabir shrugged, as if leaving it entirely on her to decide. He knew he being was over-optimistic about it but there was no harm in trying even if it was just a long shot. It just felt so nice talking to her!

Ever been to those games when the teams are called in again because one of the teams challenged the previous decision and the contest is held once more. And then the next time around the other team wins. That was the capricious state of affairs in the judging panel inside Lucia's head. Meanwhile Kabir stood outside, oblivious to the inner happenings like the supporters who couldn't get the tickets to the stadium and can only guess the happenings by the noise erupting from the stadium.

"Okay, fine, I will postpone if you sing for me." As those words escaped Lucia's lips she broke into a smile. Inside she wondered who said those words, was somebody putting words into my mouth, she wondered.

"What if I sing and you fall in love and wanna settle down, then? Relax! I just want you to postpone your flight not settle down…" Kabir said as a matter of fact, with a big smile in his eyes. He was surprised by his confidence.

"Then don't sing!" Lucia laughed. She felt it wouldn't be too bad an idea spending a day with him. As she saw him absorbed tackling his food with a fork and a knife with surprising dexterity, she wondered whether he didn't care.

"What?" Kabir looked up at her smiling at him.

"I don't know… spending a day like that with a stranger…"

"In fact, its best because it is with a stranger. When you are with somebody you know, you are stuck with them but not with a stranger. No senorita, you can say goodbye to them anytime. You don't owe them anything! Perhaps a goodbye but that's it!" Kabir could provide convincing logic for everything. He had the gift of the gab. We all have gifts that make us who we are. Those gifts are not to compete with each other but to just be happy.

Lucia had the gift of poise. And this poise demanded attention.

"What? Oh, come on! What are you thinking?" Kabir spoke with his eyes as much as with words. His eyes earnest and curious, dilating with hope. It was the cocktail for the day.

Twenty One

NOW LUCIA WAS not the one to make impulsive decisions but this whole trip in India had been nothing but impulsive bringing a tectonic shift in her thinking, the aftereffects of it would resonate in her decision making for times to come.

Later, when asked why she had decided to spend the day with Kabir, she would attribute it to logic which was not entirely true. It had made sense whatever Kabir had said about strangers (remembering it would make her smile). And that she would have just sat at the airport otherwise, but choosing the other way got her to see a bit of Mumbai. But it was because deep inside she knew that she had learnt to let go and to be okay to not be in control of everything all the time.

"Nothing, just that we can't be carrying the bag like this if we are to discover the city." Lucia said, thinking all she had to do was to reach the airport on time for the flight. She made a mental note to reach two hours in advance for her 8 o'clock flight.

Kabir didn't let Lucia pay the bill. It was not a big amount anyway, and he argued that he had made Lucia walk. The Irani cafes are decently priced, but it had more to do with the Indian mentality of not letting a guest pay.

Indians have an authority in bargaining and have been made to come across as cheap by some comedians, but when it comes down to paying in restaurants perhaps there cannot be any
more generous.

At most social gatherings in India, when it comes to paying the bill, there is always a bit of a tussle, much like the internal tug of war, as to who gets to pay for it, with each party emphatically vying for the waiter's attention. And quite like the internal tug of war of decision making, here too the decision has been made but an ostentatious display of games is to calm the nerves of the host and the guest. (People resort to extraordinary measures that may include snatching the bill from the waiter's hand before it is even laid on the table. It's like a Mexican standoff but funnier and louder. Mostly undertaken by husbands, and like most Indian activities, the whole family participates in it. While wives cheer them on from the side lines, children act like cheeky scouts who sneak off to cash counter unless ambushed. It's quite a spectacle.)

Twenty Two

KABIR WAVED IN the air, an auto stopped and the three of them got in. The rucksack took as much space as a person. The yellow-black *three-wheeler* or *autos* as they are fondly called in India are one of the mainstays of public transport in any Indian city. There are no seat belts in it, and neither has doors. Lucia got in first, the bag between the two of them, and then Kabir sat with his bum barely managing to fit in. He joked about how much their bag had grown over the years. And reprimanded himself for making a silly remark. And to compensate, he had to say something.

"So the plan is, we can drop it off at my friend's place. She would be happy to keep it for us." Kabir made sure that Lucia heard it was a female friend. He thought it'd be a little more comforting for Lucia as he was a stranger to her after all. He cringed at the thought of being just a stranger to her and wished secretly to be the song of her life. To compensate for the lack of intimacy, Kabir resorted to a commentary explaining everything about autos.

The need for an auto arose in India as most people can't afford a car and public transport . And in small towns you can see them carrying twice or even thrice their authorised capacity of three passengers. Even the driver's seat is shared with passengers and sometimes just the bare minimum of butts touch the seat. It's funny yet admirable to see how so many people are crammed into so little space, and with little complaint. While on the other side, you have people in flights sitting in adjoining seats playing territorial games over the armrests like India and China.

Kabir spoke endlessly and Lucia listened tirelessly. India is a country of contrasts Lucia thought and created a mental palette of contrast to use later to draw from her memories.

Twenty Three

"YOU ARE NOT asking him the cost of the ride?"

"Oh, you have a meter here..."

"And they follow it..."

"Yeah."

"Wow... Every time I took it they were like asking too much money!"

"Really?"

"Maybe because I'm a foreigner?"

"In Mumbai?"

"No, in Jaipur, or Varanasi..."

"Ah, well, in the rest of India they mostly don't follow the meter, in fact to them I'm a foreigner too!" Kabir quipped, winking at Lucia as he pointed at the fare meter. He found the thought of being considered a foreigner in his own country amusing. It was the first time he had put it into words. At first the thought left him with an after taste of feeling alienated, that struck a chord with the void inside him. This minor chord went unnoticed, for now only making him quiet. Unrelenting it would reveal itself much later as a full blown symphony.

The auto driver was in his late fifties with a flowing white beard and a netted skull cap that did an inadequate job of hiding his baldness but then again that was not its purpose. His forehead had a soot coloured mark of forbearance towards God developed over the years by repeated prostration. He had the aura of a content person. And he sang along the songs playing on YouTube on his phone, all the while he was driving, giving the impression that the auto was fuelled by his songs. There was no swearing, nor sudden changes in octave, even if someone cut him off. Just a lazy sideways shake of his head to dismiss the act.

There wasn't much conversation in the usual sense. Kabir and Lucia would glance at each other, smile, and pull away, like the waves of a morning sea silting the beach leaving their gentle marks.

Kabir had not met a woman like Lucia and not like this. She looked so beautiful. Like a boy who has found the most wondrous thing he looked at her trying to decipher her song. Kabir believed everybody had a song playing in their head all the time. Some were aware of it, and some were not. The serendipitous meeting had lent Lucia a magical touch and to him a magic carpet to soar above his worries. What a beautiful day he thought to himself, his heart was singing just like the old man who was singing a melodious old Bollywood song with a line that was rather philosophical—

*"I kept walking hand in hand with life,
and blew all the worries in smoke."*

Soon enough Kabir was singing along with him. It started with a hum but soon enough he was singing out aloud pondering how much he was sure to miss this city and would he ever come back here again. Probably not, he mused, shaking his head. And the song and this company made it easier to bear the burden of saying goodbye to a city that had shown him a dream. His shoulders relaxed and he smiled and allowed the music to carry him through. His voice floating at first, infused the air with his essence and in turn everyone who was breathing that air.

Twenty Four

MOST PEOPLE THOUGHT the weather and traffic were tough to deal with in India. For Lucia it was neither of those two. It was the rampant poverty that made her heart break. Ghoulish hands of destitution preying on children and adults alike. It would transfix her mind, stopping everything, making everything in her brain stationary as if all the neurons had forgotten to fire. A feeling of helplessness would pervade her every moment. She was perplexed as to how Indians dealt with it.

Lucia was enjoying the old man singing. She liked this happy vibe in the air, and it allowed her to look and assimilate. It helped her shift focus off the poverty of the street urchins selling colourful things and onto their silly antics and genuine smiles. As they stopped at a traffic signal a couple of them came to her. They were addressing her in English.

"Ten rupees, didi... Okay, five rupees..."

She wasn't going to give them any money, but she did have a packet of biscuits and gave it to them along with her best smile. The children don't need much to be happy. Little gestures are well appreciated by them.

Lucia's ear picked on a new voice singing and the underlying pathos in it made her heart swoon. Lucia glanced sideways to find Kabir singing. He was somewhere else and didn't see her noticing him, absorbed as he was in his thoughts. She could make out he was physically there but not quite present. She liked his voice instantly. It had a rare calming quality. Curiously enough, she had felt relaxed in his presence right from the very beginning and she wondered now whether it was the effect of his voice. He was a baritone but was hitting the higher notes as ably as a tenor. She was not an expert in singing but it didn't matter. Soon enough Lucia felt more of Kabir's comforting presence permeating into her. He was not like any other Indian man she had met. In fact, he wasn't like any other man she had met anywhere. She still hadn't been much able to pigeonhole him as a certain type and she now didn't feel the need to. It's a natural tendency for everyone to define a person, especially a stranger, it makes them less intimidating. She didn't feel this need anymore.

Kabir's song was much like the sunlight falling through the trees, lighting the path between the shadows. To Lucia it made the otherwise deplorable streets filled with the vicissitudes of life less painful to look at. And she afforded to give away a kind smile to the less fortunate ones while they tugged at her. She opened the strings of her heart and not the purse which was easier.

Then it occurred to her that maybe it was the music which made it all bearable.

Twenty Five

THE OLD DRIVER was enjoying Kabir's harmonious voice too.

"Are you a singer?" the old man asked looking through the rear view mirror.

"Sometimes... sometimes," replied Kabir.

"Stop! Stop here!" Kabir tapped the old man's shoulder to stop.

They had arrived and Kabir leaped out of the rickshaw. Kabir asked the old man to stay put for five minutes. The driver switched the ignition off, but a new song had started playing and he simply nodded in return, humming the new tune. Kabir and Lucia were out of the time capsule. And the staccato sounds of *damru* started to take over.

Five minutes in India are never five minutes. Five minutes could be any length of time, it is just a euphemism for 'time'. Everyone is aware of it, yet everyone believes it every time.

Twenty Six

LUCIA FELT BEING pushed forward in time as they got out of the auto. The old driver had somehow managed to keep the effects of the time capsule intact but now that they were out of it, the time had regained its speed. In fact, now she felt its effect twice as fast, almost as if time was trying to make up for the earlier slow moments. They were traveling through space and time. Lucia became aware of it. Call it the woman's intuition. She noticed it first in the nervous energy about Kabir whose actions were playing catch up.

She thought about the lives of people who lived here, the unwanted attention she was drawing from the passers-by, by just being there. When they looked at Lucia people slowed down their pace or stopped doing what they were up to, and when she wasn't visible any longer , they were jerked back into their respective 'time zones'. In a way she was slowing down time for them. The thought amused her. Oh Dali! Persistence of time…

Simi lived in a flat in one of the many cooperative housing societies in Mumbai. She was from Mumbai and had become a close friend of Kabir during his time here.

She was a singer herself. But Kabir didn't explain these to Lucia, his thoughts were more on the lines of what they would do after the bag had been taken care of. Where would they go? What places might Lucia like? What does she do? Why hadn't he asked her that yet? A nervous excitement reverberating from the drum of his heart was leaking out in small measures. Unlike Lucia, he was occupied by thoughts of the future, which prevented him from being aware of the tricks time was playing with him. Maybe it's because women are intuitive making them more immune to time. Perhaps that's why they live longer than men.

Twenty Seven

AS THEY ENTERED through the big wooden gate of the society, Kabir took out his phone and called Simi. The wood of the gate had gone black in a lot of places, as if it had seen many years and possibly even a few days such as this when the *damru* makes people dance.

"*We have entered the building... yeah we... Yes, there's an urgency... Come soon...*" Kabir hurriedly spoke in Hindi and disconnected the call. He didn't want Lucia to feel left out, who though was more comfortable than he knew.

"Simi will take the bag, hopefully. She lives in that flat." Kabir pointed to one on the seventh floor.

The society consisted of two adjoining seven-storied buildings. It was the usual height for most buildings that were constructed about twenty or thirty years ago. They had been given unimaginative names, A and B, which was quite unusual. There was a small garden in the society premises that was soothing equally for the eyes and the lungs.

Simi came rushing, twisting her medium length hair in a bun as she walked out of the lift. She had a round face and though otherwise gentle, her small eyes lent her face a misguiding stern look. She looked frail but exuded an inner strength. Kabir spotted her from where they were and with arms wide open, called out —

"Simi!"

Simi had been in front of the mirror admiring herself when Kabir's call had come through. Mirrors tend to slow down time just like phone calls tend to make them go fast. It's a secret very few people know and only those who do, can be immune to it. Simi was not one of those people.

There was this nervous excitement around Kabir which would make the whole conversation a quick one. This excitement was affecting Simi a bit too, but Lucia was pretty immune to it just then, feeling amused more than anything else. Time was playing the *damru*, Kabir was prancing to it. And now it was time for the *damru* to make Simi dance too.

Twenty Eight

"*KABIR, WHAT'S THE urgency... I was getting ready!*" Simi spoke in Hindi, a little cross. She was wearing a loose tee-shirt tied in a knot, a pair of jeans, and loafers. She looked like someone who was getting dressed but had been interrupted. It was her hair that gave her away.

"*Arey.. you are as it is so beautiful, what do you need to get ready for!*" Kabir was good with compliments, it softened Simi's eyes.

"*And she is the urgency.*" Kabir gestured towards Lucia.

"*Who is she?*" Simi's eyes widened, and she gaped at Lucia, her expression surpassing astonishment.

"Lucia meet Simi, Simi meet Lucia" Kabir moved enterprisingly, his voice dazzling, his eyes beaming.

"Hi, nice to meet you," said Lucia with a polite smile.

"Hi, yes, yes... same here!" Simi gushed while her eyes flashed her amazement at Kabir.

"*Very beautiful she is... Where did you find her?*"

"*Yes, isn't she? Nothing to it, just Rang De Basanti happening with me.*" Kabir made a proverbial reference to the cult film in which the popular actor Aamir Khan plays a Punjabi character trying to woo a British lady visiting India.

Time was playing the *damru,* announcing – Dance, my dear birdie, and you shall be rewarded. And Kabir did the dance.

"Oh, I'm telling her that this is your first time here in Mumbai. Right?" Kabir spoke fast, compensating for leaving Lucia out of the conversation till then.

"Oh, yes, yes... First time in India," said Lucia with schoolgirl sincerity.

"Oh, nice... welcome, welcome. You wanna come up and have some food?" Simi bypassed Kabir and couldn't help but dance along. She stepped towards Lucia, who had become the centre of her attention and the proverbial guest from the timeless Indian proverb 'guests are God' and Gods have to be always propitiated. But before Lucia could reply, Kabir quickly jumped back in the saddle of the conversation.

The *damru* is a small drum that Lord Shiva holds, making the universe dance to its beat. It plays at a certain tempo but has certain rapid beats in quick succession that could signify a change among other things. And Kabir was playing catch-up to the tune whenever that happened.

Twenty Nine

"*YOU ARE NOT even allowing the dal to cook... and you want to serve food already? It's her last day in Mumbai... she has a flight in the evening...*"

"Oh... *Then why did you call me?*"

"Oh, yeah! Can you please keep her bag until this evening?" requested Kabir.

"No?" Simi had learned the art of saying an immediate 'No' to every request made and then decide whether she wanted to do it or not. Always.

"Please nah, Simi... You just have to carry it in the lift..."

Simi thought about it and that was Kabir's cue to hand the bag to her who didn't expect it to be quite that heavy.

"*It's so heavy!*"

"*Arey... you have biceps – triceps... You even go to the gym!*"

Kabir's gift of the gab was good enough to coax Simi into agreeing however reluctantly. Plus the *damru* had not given her much time to think.

"*Achha, now suggest where should we go... where can we spend the day?*"

It's at this point that Simi finally felt the tricks of time. Call it the female's intuition, but Simi first kept the bag down, and in doing so stopped time. And just as Lucia, Simi too stopped listening to the *damru* anymore. Whatever the reason, Simi gave herself a few seconds of deep thought and when she spoke, it was accompanied by a snap of fingers; maybe the snap stopped the *damru* altogether.

"*Town is an option to go...*"

Town was the popular name given to the *real Bombay* that comprised five islands, which was connected by reclaimed land. The Mumbai that existed before the rest of the suburbs popped up like broccoli that nobody liked but everyone ate.

"Oh, yeah that's a good idea. You have not been to town, have you?" Kabir wondered why it hadn't occurred to him.

"No, I haven't been anywhere in Mumbai," Lucia said piteously.

"Okay, great, then you'll love it."

"Shall I give this bag too?" Lucia removed Kabir's Quechua knapsack that she was wearing to hand it to Simi.

"Yeah, yeah, give it... I'll take it," Simi replied earnestly in her more-than-happy-to-help mode.

"*Arey,* no baba, that's mine. I'll keep it." Kabir quickly grabbed the bag and strapped it on his back, quite in tune with the sounds of the *damru*. He helped Simi lift Lucia's bag as it was a bit heavy for the light frame Simi.

"Thank you, yaar... I love you!" exclaimed Kabir.

"And I hate you!" Simi replied but of course she didn't mean it.

Kabir saw Simi waddle with the bag towards her lift. And he made a dash towards the auto waiting for them. The *damru* by now had reached its zenith at this point.

Thirty

IF IT'S ONE thing that annoys the *autowallahs,* its waiting for a customer. Even though the meter is running when they wait, they always feel they can earn more not waiting. And now because Kabir and Lucia were going to town they wouldn't be requiring the auto, Kabir would have to let the singing autowallah go after making him wait. Autorickshaws were not allowed in the town area, only cars were. A rather subtle division of class. The colonial legacy was alive but perhaps only in subtle ways. In the British Raj the poor were exploited rather grossly but now it's more subtle. People assume freedom was won but only the word 'subtle' was won in struggle for independence.

Before Independence when the Britishers governed India, they had put up several deprecating boards outside clubs and other places that read – Indians and Dogs not allowed. Nothing subtle about it. And now after independence certain breeds of Indians had climbed up the so-called social ladder but surprisingly, certain breeds of dogs too had surpassed people on the social ladder. And there happen to be several places that welcome dogs but not people although the boards have been changed to – 'Rights of Admission reserved'. But it's all done subtly. Some Indians have been reposing faith in fairness creams to become the new *Gora,* though thankfully, without much success. But that's a different story with a different tune for a different time.

For now the *damru* was still beating against Kabir's ribs, pumping blood at a rate that could make a dead man dance.

Kabir gave the autowallah some extra money as compensation for having to wait and then let him go. It softened the old man's mood, who had stopped singing. He now smiled and Kabir breathed again. The *damru f*aded away for now but not before a little outro.

Lucia rushed out as she saw the auto going away. She was in no mood to walk.

"Hey auto, no wait!"

"What happened?"

"Why did you let the auto go, I don't wanna walk anymore!" whined Lucia.

"No, we won't have to walk, I'm booking an Uber. Because autos don't go there." Kabir grinned at Lucia's whose face gave him a momentary insight into how she must have been as a child. It's the first encounter with adoration you feel for the other, when you get a glimpse of their inner child.

"Okay, so we don't have to walk anymore," said Lucia who could be surprisingly credulous at times. It was a virtue, but it had also brought her pain in the past. It had also brought her to India. If you look closely at somebody and give them enough attention you can always see the child beneath the layers of blanket the society throws over at them. These blankets more often than not insulate people from themselves. And if Kabir had not been so mesmerized by her, he would have been able to see her pain carefully hidden. It would take a while for his eyes to adjust to the dazzle and see clearly. Meanwhile, the looming *damru* was an unconscious distraction which had yet to be prevailed over.

Thirty One

KABIR'S HEART WAS figuring out a way to pump blood at relatively slower rate, Lucia's brain was levelling the pitch for the next tug of war whenever it would happen, and the Uber driver was figuring out, albeit in vain, to find a way to reach them. The car was moving in circles trapped in the app on a phone, in what looked like a puzzle that a two-year old could solve without lifting her finger from the screen.

Kabir and Lucia chose to rescue the Uber driver from his impending existential angst by deciding to walk to meet the cab at a more accessible point. They used a shorter route that was via a dusty little lane lined up with several trees, blossoming with yellow flowers. The songs of several birds greeted them as they walked through this tunnel in the space-time continuum, unperturbed by the civilization honking in agony in a distant universe. Meanwhile, the Uber driver began to hear the *damru*. Only if he knew when to say 'Jumanji' he would be saved.

Kabir could say the most unpredictable of things and make it sound most obvious. The secret lay in expressing oneself honestly. It's a skill like any other but something Kabir had been born with.

"You guys have strong calves. I mean you guys walk a lot. And by 'you guys' I mean everyone in Europe. Walking here in India is still considered a necessity of the impoverished or a prescription by the doctor."

Nobody till now had ever said anything of her calves to Lucia. But she stopped for a moment to secretly check if her calves were really strong. She found them strong although wished them to be slimmer. Her mind then flew to all the calves that she had seen or remembered. It was a strangely correct observation.

"Yeah, we do have strong calves but that doesn't mean we don't get tired," said Lucia with a little pride on having discovered something new.

"Yeah, ok... But here in India like we take a scooter or an auto even for short distance but in Europe I saw people walking so much all the time."

"Okay, I'm walking, I'm not complaining!"

Kabir laughed at this.

"So what do you think of India?" Kabir knew everyone liked India, but he wanted to know what she thought of Indians or specifically what she thought of him. He wanted to know everything, but he knew it was not an easy ask. And he wasn't going to ask her directly. Kabir could be tactful when he wanted to be but then again, women could be so subtle at times almost secretive that it was hard to decipher what was on their minds. He remembered her friend replying to his query about what's on her mind,

"Sometimes even we don't know what's on our mind." And then he wondered how he too felt that, and he used music to express it. And then his mind drifted to the scriptures saying there's a feminine side in every man too. Perhaps that's why people indulge in arts. To decipher what the woman in them is saying. Lao Tse referred to it as the female mystery. Kabir wondered if art would be the way to understand Lucia too.

"India is warm and there are a lot of warm hearted people here." Lucia had a coy way of smiling that accentuated her large eyes. It was a subtle expression, but its effect was not subtle at all. It echoed as a spring in Kabir's step as if all those words were just for him.

"Oh, yes, we are very warm hearted people. We are like little Suns!" Kabir looked up with a certain pride in his voice. He believed one day we will all become a sun, selflessly serving others. He had always felt a strange association with the sun.

Their brief glances carried secret messages to each other which their hearts would take time to decipher. The Uber driver had meanwhile given up on the puzzle and now stood motionless, waiting.

Thirty Two

SOMETIMES KABIR FOUND silence too irresistible, and he would break it not wanting to be overwhelmed by it.

"Hey, Lucy! So what does your name mean?"

"Lucy! My grandma used to call me Lucy! Like the TV show, 'Everyone Loves Lucy'!" Lucia exclaimed, pleasantly surprised that Kabir had called her by that name. Names can work like clues, tugging at nostalgia, reminding us of who we are. Lucia had a quick rendezvous with her grandmother's 'Lucy', as her mind drifted back to her childhood and a sudden pang of longing overtook her.

"'Everyone Loves Lucy'... ahem... So yeah, what does it mean?" Kabir brought her back in the moment before she could stray too far in the chasm of memory.

"Lucia means light," she smiled. It was her grandmother who had told her that. She was going back and forth in time in the blink of an eye.

Kabir could sense that, and he had taken hold of her attention, allowing her to wander into her memories but never letting her go out too far lest nostalgia take over completely. And in that effect he had taken up the role of that rope which allows a bungee jumper to fall freely.

The time, the beats of silence didn't overwhelm Kabir, they beckoned him onward to sing along.

"Well, I bet you light up the places wherever you go."

"Are you flirting with me?" She cocked a playful eyebrow.

"I wouldn't tell you if I were."

"Okay..." Her tone complemented her eyebrow's playfulness.

"But on a serious note, what could possibly make you postpone your flight?"

"Hmm....Maybe an unforgettable experience?" Lucia said, shrugging her shoulders, enjoying this exchange.

"Well, I'll take that maybe as a strong yes!"

"You just have to remember to make me reach the airport in time!" Lucia spoke aloud, reminding herself more than Kabir that she still had a flight to catch.

"That is, if you don't change your mind..." Kabir teased.

Lucia made a face that spoke many things all at once, all of which Kabir understood.

Thirty Three

THE GAME WAS afoot, as Sherlock would have said. They stepped out of the tunnel, back into the space-time continuum, to first rescue the trapped Uber driver and then onwards to rescue each other.

Kabir gave the password to the Uber driver which was more like a key for him to get back into business. And together they went onto the great adventure across the seas, quite literally. They took the Bandra-Worli Sea Link, an impressive bridge and perhaps the only immersive engineering feat in modern India after the Bhakra-Nangal dam. The laurels of the past have become cushions to sleep on for Indians. Rarely do they rise from the slumber!

The sea breeze felt nice in her hair initially but soon enough it was making it fly all over the place. Lucia tied it up in a bun and her long slender neck reminded Kabir of a Modigliani painting.

There was a stark difference between different parts in Mumbai and there were always some slums everywhere you went. Lucia wondered how those poor people lived in the stifling heat in such areas. Her heart would always go out to the little kids, enamoured of their smiles undeterred by the surrounding poverty.

They soon crossed an area called Reclamation where many love birds roosted. All in their own frenzy of love. Kabir explained to Lucia how people in Mumbai couldn't get a private place to be together and they had no choice but to profess love out in the open. Public display of affection is scorned at in India, hence remaining clandestine was important too. Fortunately, Mumbai police was not as hellbent on making life worse for them as in many other Indian cities where sometimes the youth division of certain political parties too have taken up moral policing. Such sights reminded Kabir of his own yesteryears and his encounters with the moral police which now he could laugh at. But today was not the day to divulge them.

Finally they were in the area what Kabir was referring to as the 'town'. Lucia was reminded of the Gothic architecture she had seen in many cities of Europe. There were wider open spaces in this part of the city and the older buildings added grandeur. If the place had been cleaner and with fewer people, it could have passed off as a city in Europe.

Lucia thought, good decision to come here instead of the airport. Good *stupid* decision she corrected herself, as she saw Kabir's eyes darting away from her neck.

Thirty Four

IT WAS THE beginning of a nice sunny day and already there were plenty of tourists doing touristy stuff.

Kabir didn't want to get down in the crowd as he had no idea how comfortable Lucia would be. So he made the car stop near the kerb at the end of the street opposite the beautiful building of the Taj Mahal hotel. They got down from the cab to the sight of a few pigeons taking flight against the picturesque backdrop of the Gateway of India that stood tall, a daunting yet inviting giant, with the noisy and sweaty throngs around its legs. Lucia got a good photo with her phone.

They strolled along the road towards the Gateway that was dwarfed only by the vast expanse of the sea. The waters around the gate were murky with a lot of boats nestling peacefully.

"This water doesn't look too clean."

"No, it isn't. I wish it were though. Yeah, I was reading in the newspaper the other day that if you take a dip in beaches of Mumbai you might get some skin disease or rash or something."

"Does people... Do people take dips here?" asked Lucia. Although she understood and spoke English well enough, she did struggle with the grammar sometimes, as it wasn't her first language.

"No, no they don't. It's not healthy to do so. But surprisingly people do swim in some of the beaches of Mumbai." Kabir smiled wryly; he was never getting into those waters.

"The water in and around Mumbai is not clean and mostly because of the disposal of untreated wastes dumped in it. Cleanliness unfortunately is not our first attribute. Sure, you may find some rare people these days who avoid throwing garbage or waste out on the streets... But..."

"I miss my sea in Barcelona when I'm away."

"Yeah?"

"Yeah, it is soooo blue!"

"You know once when I was in Barcelona I ended up seeing people nude there!" Kabir laughed awkwardly, remembering his embarrassment. The day was still fresh in his memory when he had gone to the beach. A mermaid wearing aviators lying topless on the beach. Never had he seen a beautiful woman sunbathing like that with her breasts out in the open. The sunbathing mermaid had raised an eyebrow back at the sailor boy making him realize he had been staring at her. He had rebuked himself that day for staring and today again for mentioning the nude part.

"Because you went to a nude beach?" Lucia jumped at him with a finger pointing and a raised eyebrow. She was excited that Kabir had been to her city. But whether she was going to let him know that depended on his response.

Kabir fumbled for words, grappling with embarrassment caused by Lucia's finger still pointing like a moral pistol and the raised eyebrow reminding him of the mermaid with the aviators.

"No, I don't know... just that there were people topless..."

"Oh, then it's okay. That's not a nude beach. Nude means completely nude!" Lucia gestured animatedly with arms going from top to bottom, laughing hard. She remembered the time when she and her friends had decided to go to a nude beach, but not a story for today. It was a funny day and so it was today to see Kabir's flustered face.

"Well, to an Indian it was nude enough!"

"Yes, yes, I'm sure!" Her tone continued to be teasing.

Thirty Five

BEFORE LUCIA COULD ask what else Kabir had seen in Barcelona, the fairness tune had made an entrant as she found herself surrounded by a big Indian family requesting a photo with her. They were probably from one of the smaller towns out for a day and for them seeing a foreigner was part of the package. The slim dark skinned ladies looked pretty in their colourful, vibrant cotton sarees. They were perhaps wearing their best clothes kept only for rare occasions. Their arms were adorned with colourful glass and plastic bangles, hands clutching their little children. The bigger kids held their father's hand who ogled awkwardly from a little distance, also dressed their best. All of these indicating that they came from a rather poor family. For them to interact with a foreigner was certainly a rare event. The women had big smiles and giggled and whispered as they interacted with each other about Lucia mostly, discussing her physical attributes. Lucia was indulgent and coddled their children, even holding one of them in her arms for the photo.

Kabir couldn't help thinking how most of the privileged people in India would not hold the poor kids in their arms for imagined concerns of hygiene or something else. But Lucia hadn't cared about that. She didn't differentiate between class, a characteristic that he found appealing.

After the group photo was done, one of the husbands deftly placed himself next to Lucia, for a solo photo with her, holding a child in his arms. Kabir, already amused, tried hard but couldn't control his laughter at how this chap had wriggled himself into position for the photo. The group left happy and satisfied with an exciting tale for times to come. Grown women giggled like schoolgirls, while their men walked ahead of them with a newfound swagger.

"Well, Lucia, now you have a family in India too!" Kabir was still laughing, amused by the innocence of the proceedings.

"You saw!" Lucia was left equally entertained as she waved back at the women who kept looking back, waving at her from the distance. Lucia had come across some jerks and loafers, groups of young men wanting to take a photo with her, and it was always uncomfortable for her. But this was different, a simple family out for a day and she had been charmed by grownups behaving like little children.

"Well, you are indeed a celebrity!"

"What can I say? At first I thought it was so weird. Like for what, just the colour of the skin?" Lucia laughed and shook her head. She found the idea of this white skin fetish ridiculous.

"And now?"

"And now I've gotten used to being a celebrity!" Lucia winked at Kabir but quickly added, "No, I'm just kidding!"

Kabir liked her sense of humour. And it didn't take much to make him laugh. It was his perfect cover.

Thirty Six

THEY WALKED PAST the Taj Mahal Hotel's grand entrance, past the public urinals that attracted as many people as the Gateway itself, past the colourful dresses and loud voices, and the heavily armed security guards. Then they split up to join the respective queues for men and women to enter the Gateway compound.

Like any crowded place in India, at the Gateway, there are special security precautions, x-ray machines for scanning bags and the bored police personnel scanning people in one fluid yet mechanical motion from top to bottom, a movement that has become second nature to them. Men were quickly frisked at these smaller security gates that beeped when someone passed through, while women walked through little cabins that protected their modesty. After passing through one such security gate, Kabir entered the Gateway's compound and waited for Lucia to join him.

Lucia had to open her bag and show the contents, the lady constable dipped her hand in the bag and out with one swift motion. She was greeted by a beaming smile from Kabir when she was out.

"And this is the gateway of India!" announced Kabir proudly in an announcer's voice.

"It looks impressive!"

Kabir read out what was written on the top, though was unsuccessful to translate the roman numerals.

"To commemorate the arrival of the King George in the year... year isn't important!"

But then Lucia translated it for him. She would end up translating for Kabir not just what he saw on the outside but also what was hidden inside neatly tucked away into far corners of his memory. That would happen much later though when Kabir would begin to open up about his feelings.

Thirty Seven

YOU FIND ARCHWAYS in a lot of the European cities like Madrid, Barcelona, Milan, Paris, and of course there was one even in New York. In India, the two most popular such gates, are the ones in New Delhi, called the India Gate, and the one in Mumbai, the Gateway of India. Both were built by the Britishers when India was their colony. The India Gate served as a war memorial and every Republic Day there was an intricate ceremony that involved wreath laying and bugles and parades and gunshots. And once a year for that brief time the martyrs were remembered.

The Gateway on the other hand had a less romantic truth and was quite literally the gateway through which the colonial masters entered India via the sea. Now although a relic of the past, it served as a photo background for social media posts as relics often do. It had grown to become a symbol of Mumbai, replacing the older Mumba Devi temple (from which the city took its name) or even the dargah of Haji Ali (that stood in the sea watching over the city like a guardian angel). The non-religious colonial Gateway attracted millions of people every year who come to the city and for good reason too. It was an impressive structure. But once the people have had their desired photograph taken, very few bother to give it a second look to admire this beautiful Indo-Saracenic architecture specimen.

'What else? What to do next?' drives these buzzing swarms of bees to the next touristy spot.

Most everyday tourists are from smaller towns and every time you go there it gives you the impression of coming to a fair in a sea of humanity. You have your daily hawker fishes, their mouths gasping and gulping to feed the milling tourists all sorts of eatables, ranging from peanuts, cottons candy, pani puri, the ubiquitous vada-pav, and others selling small toys, balloons and all those things that you never need but suddenly desire to buy. Their mouths tirelessly gulping boredom and bubbling rhyming calls gasping for your attention. The thrill of holding a photo as a tangible piece of memory has allowed the photographer with their instant cameras to thrive, despite everyone having a phone with a camera feature. These octopuses with their long tentacles brandishing photo albums, the instant cameras, printer, and several other things, all at once, tirelessly, and inexorably, pursue going from one to another, spewing their ink to create instant photos. Much like the waiters they have an excellent comic timing.

"Two for 150 rupees. It will be a memory forever."

But who could tell them that a memory forever is too cumbersome to carry these days. In this age people prefer the convenience of digital photos that could be deleted when not required. It was a reflection of modern relationships. Perhaps the octopuses could boost business by removing the 'forever'.

And sharks dart aimlessly policing the area driving away the trouble-mongers and spreading out the schools of sardines that stood without a clue. While the jelly fish roamed invisible to the rest including the sharks, preying on the pockets, picking them effortlessly. Their stings would be discovered only once you were out of the sea.

Kabir was a well-read person and not particularly proud of the fact that India had been under the rule of another country for almost 200 years. What he felt more ashamed of was that his country had not learnt the lessons from the past. They couldn't stay united then and they fought amongst themselves still. The whole gamut of unity in diversity was just something that existed on paper. He brushed aside an octopus that was clinging on.

"The British built it. You know, right? That India was under British rule. They made a bunch of buildings and stuff, but they treated us like shit, so they had to leave." He felt obliged to provide a one-line summary of the country's immediate past.

As Lucia dipped her foot into this sea of people, several eyes shifted at unimaginable angles to check out this new foreign entity. While she adjusted to the temperature, the space, the different colours, the symmetry of the Gateway, and the entropy of all the fish around, she also noticed the change in the tone of Kabir's voice when he mentioned the British rule as if something had stung his eye. What she didn't know was that it was deeply personal for him, a matter of principle. Kabir had nothing against the Britishers in particular, he just didn't like the imposition of will of one human over the other. She offered him a smile of understanding. She liked the idea of non-violence and how a nation had stood its ground on it. Although baffled when she had first read about it, what had surprised her even more was how a small country could take over this huge country. But then again, even Spanish conquistadors had managed to bring all of South America under their control. And she was not proud of the atrocities committed, the genocide her country had been part of. She paddled her flippers sticking close to Kabir, who led the way like a champion swimmer navigating through the waves of people. While the hawkers nibbled close at hand to see if they had food for them. The octopuses tried to get a feel of them with their tentacles. The rest either gave way with quick jolting movements of their fins or became dead still at the sight of this new creature into their habitat and their eyes widened every time Lucia swam by them.

Thirty Eight

"YEAH, I READ about it. And your freedom struggle."

"Oh yeah? What else did you read?"

"I read about Mahatma Gandhi, and non-violence.. And how you say... *ahimsa*..." She was impressed with herself for being able to say that.

Everyone loved Gandhi, but Kabir like many of the Indian youth was more enamoured of Bhagat Singh, the great revolutionary who was sentenced to death by the British at the tender age of 23. Yes, Gandhi had a played a role in the freedom movement but there were many others who also deserved to be recognized for their important role.

Kabir stopped and turned around facing her, his excitement entangling the octopuses just as one was about to make an entrance with 'two for 150'.

"Yes.. But do you know about Bhagat Singh?"

"Bha... Who?"

"What! You don't know Bhagat Singh!"

Kabir looked aghast. Why didn't more people know about Bhagat Singh?

"No, I'm sorry I don't know. So who was he?" Lucia was polite and rather sensitive, a trait most Europeans have Kabir believed. Maybe it developed after the two great wars or maybe it came with the growth of self-assurance in an individual. It subdued Kabir's excitement.

"Oh, he was like a very cool chap."

"Cool chap? Okay..."

"Yeah, Bhagat Singh is like the Shay Guevara of India," said Kabir, pretty pleased with the comparison he came up with. And then he thought why Bhagat Singh had not become as cool a symbol as Che Guevara had become.

"You mean Che Guevara." Lucia corrected his pronunciation.

"Yeah, exactly, in fact Bhagat Singh was born before Che Guevara, so Che Guevara is like the Bhagat Singh of South America."

"Okay!"

"Yeah, I mean they had similar socialistic ideals and were both revolutionaries." Kabir went quiet as he came up against a wall of people standing still. The sun was up and so was everyone's hand acting like a shade; they were under a mass hypnosis.

"So what did he say?"

"Nothing, just that after the gora people, I mean after the Britishers leave, there will be brown people exploiting the other brown people."

Kabir made a quick mental note to stop referring to the Britishers as *gora*.

"You mean like the divide between the rich and the poor?"

"Yeah. Exactly..."

Kabir felt Lucia understood but her statement reminded him how poor his country was, nothing close to Lucia's developed Spain. He hated the poverty and the unjust systems in place that perpetuated it. He hated how helpless he felt at changing anything. He tried to ignore this feeling which played like an instrument jarring out of tune.

There were a lot of sounds filling the air. The cries of mothers calling out to their children, who played catch me, the different hawkers occupying different wavelengths in the air (so all their voices were as clear as any), the octopuses with their 'two for 150', the husbands with the maps of sweat drawn out on the back of their shirts, calling out to the wives to walk faster, wives trailing those sweaty maps, calling out to them to slow down, the silent, giggly mischief of the newly married couples walking hand-in-hand, the gossiping girls, the catcalling guys, all floating on their designated wavelength. Above them all today was also the sound of a loudspeaker calling out what sounded like instructions. There was a shooting going on that had resulted in the mass hypnosis of the fishes, and a part of the Gateway area had been secured with ropes demarcating the area.

Thirty Nine

"HEY LOOK, THERE'S a film shoot going on," said Kabir pulling Lucia by her arm towards the wall of bystanders all gawking at the action with their palms shading their squinting eyes, eyebrows tensed as they gently rose up and down on their heels, drifting into mass hypnosis.

"Oh, my God! Don't tell me... Is it a Bollywood film shoot?" Lucia excitedly craned her neck to get a clear sight. Modigliani would have been inspired. She was pretty tall for a woman and almost as tall as most men in India and that neck gave her an added advantage. Lucia had seen a couple of Bollywood films. She relished the sight of colourful costumes, the intricate dance routines. It was not a film for her; it was a spectacle.

"It could be a Hollywood film too, I can see some white guys there." Kabir was equally excited. And in a flash all the worries of poverty had disappeared. It was the magic of movies, they made you forget and dream. Perhaps that's why cinema was so popular in India, it was a cheap form of entertainment that took you to a place where you saw life the way you wished it to be. And that's also the reason why realism in films took some time to be popular here in India. Because for the longest time the reality for an Indian was too harsh to be paid for and viewed.

"This is so cool!"

"This is like part of the Bombay experience. You know Mumbai was called Bombay earlier and that's why that B for Bollywood."

"Oh yeah, it makes sense!"

Kabir and Lucia became a part of the wall, riding up and down on their heels, using their necks to stay above the sea of heads.

What were the odds of seeing a shoot the first place he took Lucia, Kabir thought. And then he thought what were the odds of *this*... as he looked at Lucia. And he kept looking at her as if she were the most wondrous sight and then she turned around to see him looking at her like that. Their eyes met and at that moment, almost on cue, loud music played in the backdrop and there was a call for action. Kabir and Lucia for a brief moment were elsewhere, like the hero and heroine of a Bollywood film singing and dancing in a dream sequence.

The crowd of people jostled around to watch the shoot bringing Kabir and Lucia closer until they were pressing against each other. And an octopus made its entry breaking the trance.

"Two for 150, sir. Madame, excellent memory forever. Different poses..."

The trance was broken. Kabir had seen shootings before and it could be rather exhausting to watch after a while, moreover he only had the day to spend with Lucia. He didn't want to waste it. They laughed awkwardly as push came to shove leading to awkward brushes of intimacy while the octopus gasped and gulped still for the 'two for 150'. Kabir created an opening and pulled Lucia out of the area, going around to the other side of Gateway, towards the sea.

"Come, let's go!"

"Hey, what's that building?"

"Oh, that's the Taj Mahal hotel," said Kabir, steering her through the crowd with swift freestyle strokes.

"Taj Mahal hotel, really, I like this hotel," Lucia laughed.

Kabir went onto explain about the terrorist attacks that took place here in 2008. Lucia liked the small little details and trivia that Kabir included in their talk. It was never a lecture but just enough to make it informative. It showed how much he knew about his country and also betrayed his inner thoughts.

"You know, both Air India and Indian Airlines used to be run by Tata group, the same people who run this iconic hotel. Back in the day, the then prime minister said India should have an airlines. So Tata sold the airlines to India for 1 rupee. Can you believe that? And look at the business houses here now just trying to loot the people!"

"WHAT!"

"Yeah! Can you do that again?"

"What? WHAT!"

"Yeah," laughed Kabir. He saw a lot of people both men and women checking Lucia out rather unabashedly though he couldn't do much about it. It was ridiculous to watch some of the young men walk past by her with their neck turning all the way back and trying to catch her in their selfie. They were crossing the jetty behind the Gateway from where one could board the boat for Alibaugh, Elephanta Caves or the neighbouring small islands. The ticket seller went about dominating the airwaves now much like the seagulls, "Elephanta, Alibaugh Elephanta…"

Lucia was feeling the heat now and the sweat was making her hair stick to her neck. Too much time in the sea of humanity with too much noise could give a rash too. She felt she could do with a little rest now.

"What's this 'Elephanta?'"

"Oh, hahaha… Elephanta Caves are on an island. Its gonna take a while to get there and I don't want us to get late for your flight."

"No, no… It will get late."

Lucia felt somewhat assured that Kabir was aware of time, and he seemed like a genuine guy till now but so is everybody until we actually know them. A part of her was always on the alert and kept her guard up. It wasn't personal, it was part of being a woman in a world that was still learning to be fair to her.

Forty

THEY WENT PAST the star fishes accompanied by the crabs. The star fishes posed endlessly while the crabs clicked photos dutifully walking sideways left to right and right to left to cover all possible angles. They clacked their claws at anyone who came between them.

Kabir too took a couple of photos for Lucia against the backdrop of the Gateway. And that was a tick on his checklist while the group of octopuses looked at them with forlorn eyes and drooping tentacles. At the snap of photos, they scuttled away in search of new tourists.

Kabir was feeling the heat too and he thought if he was feeling thirsty then it must be definitely hot for Lucia too.

"Hey, aren't you thirsty? I could do with some water!"

"Yeah, and I could do with some shade too," replied Lucia.

"Let's get out of here!" Kabir quickened his pace, splashing bigger strokes as he pulled themselves out of the sea of humanity.

Lucia held onto his knapsack like a lifejacket as wave after wave of people kept pouring in and only let it go when they were out. Kabir grabbed a couple of water bottles from a vendor immediately offering one to Lucia who let the cool liquid quench her parched throat. The heat in Mumbai can take a toll on you even on a winter's day unless you keep hydrating yourself. The light breeze and the comfortable temperature is very deceptive as you don't feel too thirsty, but your body keeps dehydrating.

The unforgettable experience was playing on his mind and so did the beats of the damru.

Kabir had already decided the next place to visit. The sun was already on the top of their head, and it was only going to get hotter. Museum would be indoors, they would get to talk and see things. Plus, he had never been to the museum here either. And then they could do a late lunch and he would show her the Victoria Terminus which was a UNESCO world heritage site. The plan was formed to the faint sounds of damru. The jarring instrument of poverty had been forgotten and dropped.

Although the museum wasn't too far from where they stood, Kabir suddenly got inspired to take the bus as he saw one coming along. "Come on, let's go! I have to take you somewhere!"

Forty One

THEY GOT ONTO the bus like chirpy birds. Lucia was very observant, with a keen eye for details. She noticed the rickety bus as she stepped on. When she looked at people she didn't see people, she saw only eyes. The bus was filled with many, mostly sullen, eyes. The reluctant peeper, the stare downer, the side-glancer, the look away disinterested, the envy eye, the oblivious, they were all there. Most were regular travellers, but there were a few who would perhaps never sit in the same bus again. The regular ones had only eyes and even spoke with eyes. The newer ones had only mouths on them, and they even saw with their mouths. The conductor understood both the language of the eyes and of the mouth.

The driver and conductor wore khaki, much like the postman, the Policeman, the auto drivers... Khaki was the go-to colour for uniforms in India. Like the grand buildings, it was legacy of the British, who had made it fashionable. A long thread hooked to the ceiling went down the full length of the bus, connected to a bell near the driver's seat. You could pull the thread, or the conductor did, causing the bell to ding, alerting the driver to stop. A lot of the seats in the bus were marked for women. They were generally in the first half of the bus. This was a double decker bus, and it was Lucia's first time on it. She followed Kabir past the eyes and the gaping mouths onto the upper floor. It was surprisingly empty.

Forty Two

"ARE WE GONNA sit upstairs?"

"Of course!" said Kabir, thinking that's the whole point of double decker buses. It was not as easy to climb the stairs as he thought it would be. But the higher up you went, the more bumps you felt. The bus was sort of philosophical in that way.

Ah, so that's why most people were sitting downstairs Kabir thought to himself, helping Lucia take a seat as the bus welcomed them with an excited buck. It was his first time in double decker bus too. He had only seen them from afar without ever feeling the urge to board one. She took the window seat and Kabir sat next to her. A set of yellow flowers high on the trees stood outside waving at them. There were some leaves from the trees trying to peek into the bus, grazing the window like little children who had never seen a foreigner in their lives, curious but shy.

She had been thinking of all those eyes and the reason why people in buses are so silent. Is it because buses are a sad reminder that we have grown up and can't be kids again? Before she could rationalise further, her reverie was broken.

"You know, these double decker buses run only in Mumbai and Kolkata." Kabir said. He was pleased at this decision and looked intently almost waiting to hear a well done. The unique experience Lucia wanted playing in the head on loop, like when the needle of an old gramophone gets stuck at a point.

"So this is where you wanted to bring me?" Lucia asked. She appeared unimpressed.

He was so sure she would like it that his brain was confused and now fumbled to come up with anything witty. So he did what people do when the brains are fuzzy, he tried to explain himself.

"No, I mean we are going somewhere in this."

"Relax, I'm just kidding. I like the idea of this bus," Lucia said, shaking Kabir's shoulder amiably. It was there for the taking and she couldn't help it. She enjoyed this innocent expression on his face. She wouldn't have done this had she not liked him. She knew that Kabir was really trying to impress her, and it was cute. She knew there wasn't much to come out of it but the trip to India had been nothing like she thought it would be. And Kabir at the moment seemed like a nice farewell gift from India. So she allowed herself to indulge, and it did feel good to receive all the attention she was getting.

Kabir knew she had him there and he laughed along. It was also a sign that she was opening up to him. It was like being in a movie. A movie that made him forget everything else. He had no idea how this would pan out but that was the beauty of it, he was just in this moment and nothing else mattered. Voices in his head beckoned him to ask more about her lest he lose her attention.

"Hey, you never told me what do you do?"

"I teach painting," answered Lucia. She turned around to look at Kabir. She had been looking out the window till then. Mumbai looked less chaotic from up here.

"Oh, wow, wish I could paint!" Kabir loved paintings but was terrible at painting. He could only manage to draw stick figures, a detail he chose not to share.

"Yeah, I love to paint, and I'm a ballet dancer, too. You know ballet…" Lucia brought her hands up as she tried to explain what ballet was. She didn't expect people in India to know much about it.

"Yeah, of course I know ballet." Kabir scoffed. He was a musician and he loved to listen to a lot of music. A lot of western composers had composed music for ballets. And it made perfect sense now to him, the poise in her body was because she had been trained as a dancer.

"Yeah, but I don't dance professionally." Lucia said, looking away outside. She would have liked to dance professionally but to do that takes years out of your life and it was just a very tough thing to do. And of course she loved to paint as well. It was her first love.

"What? Why not?"

"Yeah, dancing professionally requires a… a lot of things…"

"Like cigarettes?" Kabir remembered reading somewhere that ballet dancers smoke a lot to stay thin.

And his brain was on overdrive, assimilating material for conversation ever since the 'Hola! Como estas' at the cafe.

"Yeah, that too!" Lucia laughed.

"So Lucia paints and dances…"

"Yeah, just like Kabir sings and writes!" Lucia responded with a smile. She noticed Kabir shrugging his shoulder in a forlorn way that didn't escape her notice. She wondered what his story was, and what lay underneath that ever smiling face.

"Yeah, we should have a band together!" Kabir was quick to change the mood.

The conductor had come for the ticket. Kabir paid for the ticket, not allowing Lucia to pay yet again. She was not used to this, and neither could she understand why he was not letting her pay. And then something caught her attention outside, some kids were selling titbits at the signal. Lucia was trying to think what she was feeling because of Kabir… She liked how well informed Kabir was and how he was making her smile a lot. She would be pleasantly surprised by funny remarks made out of the blue. It was not your funny-funny humour but just something witty or sometimes… what's that word…

Forty Three

ALL KABIR COULD think was how he really wanted to get to know her better, there was little time and he had to think of innovative ways. People don't open up so easily in a day. And days like these don't come very often; it was like a dream come true, like something out of a movie. Why does he keep comparing it to a movie. Yes that's it. Eureka! It's almost like that movie – what was the name of that movie. Then Kabir smiled to himself as it occurred to him they were sitting in a bus too. And then he remembered Joseph Murphy.

"You know one of the best ways to know somebody is through rapid fire?"

"What's that?"

"You don't know rapid fire?"

"No."

"Oh, well, I saw this movie once and the hero and heroine get on the bus, and they do it... and..."

"And no, that's not happening!"

"What? No, no... That's not what I meant!" It took a second before Kabir could get it and a few more to recover from the embarrassment. He mustered his next words deliberately, under Lucia's scrutinizing look.

"Rapid fire is asking uncomfortable questions and giving quick answers."

"Uncomfortable and quick? Como mi primera ve sexo!" Lucia grinned at her own joke.

"What?" Kabir was a bit dazed and confused by the Spanish words and the Spanish lady.

"Nothing, nothing… you don't wanna know. So umm… that means I can ask you back as well?" Lucia shifted herself to face him.

"Of course!"

"So who goes first?"

"Me," Kabir said in a matter of fact tone.

"Of course. Okay, I'm ready." Lucia was game for it. At times Kabir made her feel like a teenager.

And as if on cue, the bus, which had stopped at a signal earlier, sped forward, joining in the fun. After all a game such as this needs a neutral quizmaster, and the Bus was happy to do what Derek O'Brien did for India.

The bus had a neat way of keeping a score by measuring the seismic activity in their hearts and didn't plan on making any secrets of it. It would reflect in every little bump, jerk, turn on the road. So that the score was for all the audience to see.

This road they had embarked upon would make them both jump, stop, roll, and experience more tricks which they didn't even know of yet.

Each kept throwing questions at the other with surprising wit that were answered fast and quick. From discovering the movies that made them cry the most, to the ice creams flavours they were most likely to ban, their dream destinations, to the famous person they were most likely to assassinate, it was a know-it-all. It was a high scoring match with not a single unanswered question and the two teams were not leaving anything to chance. It would head into a tie breaker. And it was time to bring in the big guns.

"So tell me the name of your first crush, your infatuation." Kabir added that last part unsure if Lucia knew what crush meant, it was an American lingo after all.

"Well, okay. My first crush. His name was Pablo." (Just then, the bus hit a speed bump making Kabir jump out of his seat. It was to be the first of many.) "And he was in my ballet class and all the girls used to like him. He was the only guy in our class. And one day he asked me out." Lucia roller-coasted on a little trip down the memory lane. She tripped on the weightlessness of younger times and the blood rush of the first kisses. The twists and turns of the little worries that gave such big scares then and of the time when life is about dancing and preparing for the next show.

Meanwhile, Kabir's face transformed into a rickety-rackety version much like the sounds of the bus. He couldn't help getting a teeny-weenie bit uncomfortable as she started talking about Pablo and that teeny-weenie bit was enough to get him off his game. But a desperate attempt to not lose the point was on the way.

Forty Four

"WHAT?" LUCIA ASKED, casting a concerned look at Kabir.

"Oh nothing, it's just a guy doing ballet... Is like... I don't know..." ended Kabir lamely. His face contorting into a preposterous expressions under the command of the motor cortex.

Forty Five

"WHAT... WHAT'S WRONG... I like guys doing ballet. Yeah, it's a bit feminine maybe and some of them are gay..."

"Exactly."

"But I don't care. I find men doing ballet so graceful... I like to watch them dance."

The bus stopped with a sudden brake to avoid hitting something that had just turned up on the road. Or maybe because it was surprised with what Kabir replied. It started back though at a gentler pace as it took a right turn. While Kabir furtively steadied himself mentally to get back in the game and physically to avoid being pushed into Lucia who had been pressed against the bus.

Forty Six

"YOU KNOW, I can dance too!"

"Oh, really? What do you dance?" Lucia asked. Her voice had taken on a coquettish tone.

"I can do the moonwalk." Kabir said solemnly, and with all modesty, jerked his head, neck, and shifted his feet while sitting, causing both of them to break into laughter.

The bus joined in with a big bump making them both jump in their seats. Maybe it was the speed breaker or maybe it too had joined in on the fun with a belly laugh.

"Is it always gonna be like this?"

"It's gonna be a bumpy ride, yup!"

"I see. Okay, okay… It's my turn now…" Lucia scratched her nose with her thumb like a fighter ready for a bout. She was ready with her question, and she knew exactly where to aim, Kabir having set the tone. An aim to the head would be obvious and well-guarded, it would have to be the heart.

For women, it's always the mental connection that drives them, that is why they always are more interested in knowing about love. Although men too know love, it's the physical attraction that drives them forward at first, because it involves action. Lao Tse the Chinese philosopher said action through inaction is a woman's natural state of being. It's her capacity to surrender that she can completely submerge in love. For most men love remains only as one of the things because he finds it difficult to surrender. Love requires surrender and inaction that a man finds difficult, unless he is a romantic. Kabir was a romantic.

"Alright, I'm ready."

"Describe to me the first time you fell in love?" Lucia looked on with a playful glint in her eye.

"Love, I don't know if that question is applicable..." Kabir replied, feigning nonchalance.

The bus made no bones about it as they hit a few small potholes in quick succession. Love has a tendency to shake people up, for the better or worse, it depends on how one takes it. It shook both Lucia and Kabir for entirely different reasons. Lucia was aghast at hearing his response.

Perhaps it's the greatest tragedy for a woman to like a man and discover he doesn't believe in love.

Forty Seven

"WHY? DON'T YOU believe in love?" Lucia's eyebrows rose less from the jumps than for Kabir's silence.

Kabir waited for the bus to steady and for the right words to come to him. Sometimes it took time for him to discover the right words to express what he meant.

"No, I mean I do believe in love. But the love you are referring to is the romantic love and that's not love. That's just a poet's way to disguise the lust of the society. It's only when the desire to possess and the dust of lust settles that true love begins... but very few are capable of doing that..."

Kabir's eyes opened wide revealing everything that couldn't be read but just felt. Clear crystals condensed by sensitivity and the pressures of wisdom. They looked right through Lucia and for a moment she felt enveloped by that gaze. There was a silence, and some of it touched the deepest corners of her heart. She didn't know what to say in return as she felt something in her untwist. The question had seemed simpler in her head. And now she couldn't help but agree with what Kabir had said. She thought of all the times people had professed their love to her. It had felt real but had faded away.

Lucia wanted to say something, but the right words eluded her. She knew that meant it was time to listen. Patience was a virtue which she had learned to draw in her life, and one needs patience to listen. She understood one thing though: Kabir was deep waters. He was like a book that turned a different leaf the moment she felt she knew where the story was headed.

She just wasn't sure yet as to how deep she wanted to swim. Up until a certain depth one can swim with the light of knowledge shining through, but after a certain depth one is blinded not because it's dark but because the light of faith is too bright and dazzles one beyond sight.

Being brought up in a family where the talk was light and connections tended to be a little superficial, Kabir had grown to be somebody who was not out there when it came to his inner emotions and feelings. His feelings, his fears, his triumphs, his attributions, or his joys or sorrows, remained deep like the secrets of an ocean never surfacing in the midst of small talk. Such secrets yield only to someone who listens, but most children are seldom even heard. And they grow into complex adults never having been able to spread their fragrance.

Forty Eight

BEFORE LUCIA COULD prod Kabir further on the subject, he got up in a flash and beckoned her to get up.

"Come, our stop has come!"

"Already?"

Kabir put on his knapsack balancing himself with the help of the pole grabbing it in one hand. He helped Lucia to her feet by supporting her with his other arm. The bus made sure Kabir and Lucia bumped into each other awkwardly and making their descent slower. It was like the push everyone gives to that shy teenage love birds who haven't kissed yet. It's amusing for everybody and awkward for the couple. The bus had picked up speed, honking and negotiating the traffic, in a hurry to get off this road and reach its destination, like the final few moments of play before the final whistle. Eventually the bell tinkled, signalling the end of play and the bus stopped with a jerk, instinctively making the players hold each other's hands. They hopped off.

Games are not made to pick a winner but to bring people closer. The match was even. The bus had done its thing though, it had given a fair share of blood rush and excitement.

Kabir and Lucia would realize they were holding hands only when they were out of the bus where a new world awaited them, where the Gods were waiting to welcome them , where new versions of them were waiting to be born.

Forty Nine

THE ATMOSPHERE WAS reminiscent of a bazaar that one crosses before you enter a place of worship. Only here they were about to enter an exhibition gallery instead of a temple. But who could argue it was not a temple of art? Instead of candles and lamps and coconuts you had paintings and colours and sketches. Whoever said art is religion perhaps had found love in art.

There were many artists on the pavement painting, ritualistically hanging their little offerings to the Gods of art on either side of the pavement. All for sale, they came in different colours and hues. Some would be accepted by the Goddess Laxmi who bloomed on her lotus and rewarded wealth in return, and some would remain with Goddess Saraswati, who played her veena and offered condolences of learning. While some of these ordained priests of art rested under the shade of ashoka trees on their foldable chairs, sipping tea, and blowing smoke. Some were sketching portraits for the tourists who yearned to become immortal. And people sat on these foldable chairs more dutifully and silent then they had ever been in any prayer or *pooja* as they got baptized and anointed by sketch artists and caricaturists.

Walking through them all Lucia felt rejuvenated as the weight of time had rolled off her. She was in her element and her spirit flowed through the paintings like the breeze through the leaves. Oh, how she loved to be surrounded by art all the time!

Kabir loved to look at paintings too. They would often whisper new songs into his ear. But today his attention was on Lucia and her subtle reactions which spoke a language he was beginning to understand.

In Europe you could always see artists practicing their art and selling it on the street. But to find something similar in India was a pleasant surprise for Lucia. Some of the works on display were really beautiful and caught her attention.

"I love this place!"

"So you might enjoy the art gallery too."

"I have never been in an art gallery in India. Do they have any famous works here on display?"

"Yeah... well, I don't know how famous but they're mostly Indian artists. I haven't seen an MF Hussain here. And I'm not familiar with all the names."

Kabir admitted the last bit sheepishly. He made a mental note to look up some Indian painters. He didn't know the names of any other Indian painters. He just knew of Amrita Pritam and Raja Ravi Verma.

Under the shaded trees on the footpath were many small little paintings and sketches hanging on the make shifts temporary display stands on one side and the stone wall on the other. The smiling portraits of Buddha, Indian Gods and Goddesses, like Ganesha, Krishna and Radha, blessed the passers-by from their sheets of unacknowledged holiness. Alongside them were hung various windows giving glimpses of landscapes of far off and never visited places. On one side were many birds drawn who would only ever fly in imagination and then on another side were drawn feelings that had once flown and now rested.

There were people sitting on low, round metal barricades around trees that offered cool shade. Some sat tired of all the walking and rested before they would walk again, while some sat because they had nowhere to reach and watched others walk past. The gentle breeze caressed them both. The chaiwallah walked to and fro with fervour, exorcising lethargy out of everyone he came in contact with.

Fifty

AFTER CLIMBING THE steps that led into the gallery lay an exhibition hall on the left and another on the right. The one on the right was where all the paintings were displayed which they entered first.

The exhibition halls were silent, assiduously calming the forever floating population that walked around the gallery. Some who understood the language of colours delved deeper until they themselves became paintings and some walked briskly, in silence, with questions that would resonate in them later. The shower of art from all sides permeating the senses, creating new neuron connections forever transforming all. Art exonerates, gently, and the transformation it creates is radical.

Lucia and Kabir became as children when they stepped in. They listened to the beautiful paintings and questioned the abstract shapes of design. Silence ensued between them for a while as both embarked on their own paths. The silence broke only when one of them found something unusually compelling and was driven to share with the other. Time too took a break from its clockwork existence and seemed to travel differently in this space.

There was a collection showcasing rural life of India that really fascinated Lucia. They were made with big outlines, bold strokes, and even odd shapes, yet there was a sense of beauty in that rawness. Kabir told her about the different names of tools and the folk musical instruments showcased in them. Lucia was pleasantly surprised by the skill of Indian painters, and she made a mental note to check them out later. She went onto explain Kabir about different brush strokes and what they meant. He listened to her speak about art and he still listened to her even when she had stopped speaking, all the while looking at her eyes which glistened. They reflected back something that could be best described as comfort. There was no other sound, and the stillness beckoned him to break this spell.

Fifty One

"I WANT TO look at you when you paint."

"Okayyy..."

Lucia's brain immediately drew a picture of her painting in her studio, being watched by Kabir. It occurred to her that words like colours have magic and what makes a moment magical is the existence of the revealed along with the hidden.

She didn't know that she had pictured herself just the way Kabir had imagined her. He didn't know the magic his words were creating. He was under the enchantment of colours.

Lucia shifted the focus off her.

"You never answered my question."

"What question?"

"The question about love."

"You know I feel it's quite difficult to describe love. Love is like..."

"Art."

"Yeah, you can say that... it's either nothing or everything. But you know what I don't understand is people loving and unloving. How can you *unlove*?", Kabir said it in an over casual manner like people do when trying to make it appear they are unaffected.

"Sounds like a heartbreak and nothing like art to make you heal better..." Lucia did a little twirl like a ballerina at the end of it. She had a smirk that said – I know.

"Yeah, well, I brought you here because I thought you would love the place!" Kabir's defences came up the moment someone got too close.

"But I do. I love it so much, Kabir. Thank you for bringing me here." Lucia gave a smile that pierced through those defences. Kabir melted and recrystallized in an instant.

The space around them was changing while time continued to be still. Just like time impacts the way life is perceived, the space too influences the paradigm of life.

Fifty Two

THEY HAD ENTERED the hall on the left now which was exhibiting a work of conceptual art. There were black drapes on the walls, lit with minimalistic yellow lighting strategically illuminating the space. There was a soft, light instrumental music playing in the background. The combination of it all made this space ethereal.

The high ceilings of the hall had been divided into two sections. The first section had a few stools placed facing a visual screen in the centre, with transcendental visualisations changing shape and hues. Having a hypnotic effect on anyone who looked at them. Some ten, odd looking smooth stones the size of a brick that resembled over-sized seeds, balanced on curvy iron rods, stood between the screen and the stools. Each seed on each such rod looked like an alien figure out of a doodle book. A lady sat a desk to provide information on the installation and the artists for anyone curious to know.

Both Kabir and Lucia instantly felt even more relaxed in this space. They looked around with an inquisitiveness that seemed to have wiped out all notions of memory. As they moved to the other section they saw a huge brass structure placed in the centre. It was the size of two king sized beds. The lighting, placed strategically, brilliantly illuminated the brass display in the dark space.

"Is it a toilet?" asked Lucia incredulously.

"And the biggest one I have ever seen!" Kabir controlled his laugh as some people crossed by.

Both Lucia and Kabir exchanged amused glances while others passed them carrying a serious cloud over their thoughts. These others came from all walks of life. From housewives who waddled like mother ducks in sarees, preceded by their bellies, and their kids, followed by their dutiful husbands who could be heard trying to answer improbable questions, the groups of college kids bunking classes, engrossed in taking selfies, to the lone art enthusiasts with keen eyes.

The giant toilet had a silencing effect on them all including Kabir and Lucia . Much like the silence that follows whenever truth has been spoken. Even the kids who were earlier running rampant had become soundless and held their mothers' hands. The question-answering husbands had now questions of their own, floating in their heads. And inflated balloons of ego who hovered over the rest, deflated, letting out their air in silence. The cackling groups of geese that flew in excitedly now walked with solemn steps. The rest of the farm animals all had quietened being reminded of their daily thought provoking moments. Kabir and Lucia were not immune to the effects of the space. They all watched their little ripples of thought die to give a clear view of themselves.

There was a certain gravity, a seriousness of business in thought, a sense of mindfulness that had floored all the living and the unliving.

The lady at the front desk informed that the idea behind this creation was to highlight how in the toilet, the mind is quiet, concentrated and ideas like little seeds form in the head. Apart from the more obvious aspect that the toilet is a great equalizer. Everyone goes there no matter who they are.

Fifty Three

"WELL, SHE DOES have a point, you know when I used to study during engineering exams, I always found my concentration level was high when I studied sitting on the throne," said Kabir in a forced whisper.

"I have never tried that but wait, so you are an engineer too?"

"Oh, yeah, had to study that. And thanks to the toilets, made it through."

"Wow! Incredible "

"Yeah!"

"No, I mean so you are an engineer as well…"

"It's not a big deal…"

Kabir's words trailed off, as he drifted slowly, his thoughts transitioning him into his distant past. And, perhaps for the first time, he saw his own fears behind the decisions that he had made. He knew nobody else could be held responsible for the life he had chosen.

Some people don't understand the need to cut off from the world. Lucia had spent so much time by herself that she understood this feeling. She had learned to let people be when they need their time alone. Kabir needed that time. Lucia walked ahead to check out the rest of the installation.

On one of the walls there were petri dishes about the size of a palm containing two or three polished shiny stones that resembled germinating seeds. There were numerous such petri dishes on a number of racks from zero to infinity. Every little stone represented an idea. Every idea had a smooth, polished surface.

Kabir had walked over to the other corner towards a wooden cot knitted out in jute and sat down on it. He had yet not returned and was transitioning through the clear flow chart of his life. Lucia stood absorbed in her own thoughts, of what Kabir had said of love. It made her question her own attachments, to the ghosts of her past. The yellow light glowing around her gave her a mystical aura, helping bring back Kabir to the present.

He took out his phone to take a photo of Lucia. It was an attempt to demystify the moment.

"Hey, you know, I think I can be a good conceptual artist!"

"Because you can make anyyyyything and can talk about it." Lucia spoke in a sing-song tone accompanied by a twirl that underscored her words.

"Yeah..."

Lucia turned around to see Kabir taking her photograph.

"Kabir! What are you doing?"

"Capturing time and beauty."

Kabir continued to take a few more photos, as Lucia posed, blushing. She wondered at his amazing felicity to come up with these lines that went straight to her heart and made her swoon.

"You know, I like how one person's art can inspire others to create art." Lucia was doing little dance steps with her feet as she moved about in this space.

"I like how art allows you to travel through time…"

Kabir walked up to Lucia and showed her the pictures that he had taken of her.

"See old Lucy meet new Lucy. She's saying hi to you!"

"Hi!" Lucia couldn't help being impressed by Kabir's poetic remarks and his creative mind. It all felt so refreshing.

"I like it, it's lovely!" Lucia liked the framing and the lighting. Kabir had captured something very natural, and she noticed how well poised she stood.

"Now would you be kind enough to return the favour?" Kabir offered her his phone with a smile.

Lucia had spaced out for a moment there and realised he was asking her to take his photo.

"Oh, sure! But I'll take with mine…"

Kabir was really clumsy when it came to posing for photographs. He started making weird expressions and poses that seemed forced while Lucia wondered if he was just joking but then it struck her that he was actually earnest in his efforts.

Fifty Four

"KABIR, WHAT INSPIRES you to write?" Lucia saw Kabir's comic guard fall away and there, in her frame, a vulnerable artist began to speak.

"I don't know, words just come to me you know... they... They just flow from somewhere and I... I just can't help but write them down. It's almost as if it's my duty to put them in perspective. Sometimes they come with a tune and often they have to be interpreted and require me to be attentive. And the more attentive I become, the clearer the tune." Kabir swept away from time and space floating on the words he spoke, his mind relaxed and his body started to flow, and he forgot he was being photographed.

Lucia smiled as she captured a little of him forever to be. She was happy with the result and was looking at the photos when Kabir tiptoed to her.

"Show me."

"There, you see the difference?" Lucia swiped between two photographs, showing him the contrast of where he was posing and when he just was being himself.

"I like this... Here I'm looking a bit fat..." Kabir became a little conscious of his looks, more so because Lucia looked very pretty. He had a bit of anxiety about him which would leak out in his insipid words about himself. One of the reasons for his anxiety was living in the city. Being in nature and all by himself, he was more at peace and less anxious. But the city was merely a trigger, the real cause went longer back still to his growing up where he had little space to express himself. Lucia was having a pacifying effect on him, it was allowing him to be.

"Nooo... I think here you look very relaxed."

"You know, this place is pretty trippy, like if someone had LSD or something, they would go bonkers here."

"Oh yeah. It's definitely trippy."

"Lucy and the sky with diamonds," Kabir started singing the Beatles song.

"It's 'Lucy in the Sky with Diamonds...' You know that song is about LSD..."

"That song is about Lucy. And come on let's go."

"Already?"

"Yeah, I have places for you to see and somebody still has a flight to catch!" Kabir did a little dance step of his own.

"Okay, okay..."

Kabir zipped past pulling Lucia with her as they went out of the gallery. Their eyes took a while adjusting to the daylight just as the surroundings would take a while to adjust to two free spirits.

Fifty Five

A MAN WITH a white beard sat right outside at the left entrance of the gallery. The man was likely in his 50s but looked much older. Some people age faster because they have absorbed more during the same time. His tanned skin folded happy memories in the wrinkles. He was wearing a faded polo shirt with blue and white horizontal broad stripes which had holes that ventilated his belly, and with an old, faded brown trousers that stretched when he breathed deeper. He was wearing worn out rubber soled *chappals* that had walked many miles.

The old man called out to Lucia a few times as they were getting out. She looked at Kabir quizzically. The old man gestured with his hands that he wanted to paint Lucia.

"He wants to sketch you I guess."

"Do we have time?" The thought of having a sketch drawn in India excited her. In Barcelona she used to go out sometimes when she was a student and draw portraits. It a was good Sunday practice routine. But being on the other side was exciting especially in a country like India, she found it charming. Portraits, Lucia believed, always showed how the world perceived you, unlike mirrors that showed how you looked at yourself.

"Sure if you want to..." Lucia was sitting poised in front of the man even before Kabir could complete the sentence.

"What country?" asked the old man conversationally in his broken English.

"Spain." Lucia answered charmingly.

"Very good, very good..."

"You know about Spain?" she asked, adjusting her hair on one side.

"Europe..." the old man said and gestured at her to be quiet as he started to draw the outlines.

"So how does it feel to be sketched?" Kabir stood leaning on a pole next to them, rather amused by the whole proceedings. Lucia was a bit self-conscious and couldn't help smiling all the time.

"I don't know I'm liking it..." said Lucia.

"Ssshh... no move!" the old man shushed, quite serious.

"Sorry."

"No talk." The old man went into his prayer mode and between Lucia and his sketch pad, a continuous synchronous, mechanized motion ensued that soon started drawing people closer as an amused Kabir looked on. His eyes were transfixed on Lucia who would have soon the attention of a crowd of fifty people, all staring at the old man drawing and Lucia, who sat like a deity with a fixed smile. Her lips quivering ever so slightly, her eyes dripping with shyness, she became attentive of the ever increasing attention. The eyes of the crowd moved like the spectators at a tennis match, alternating between Lucia and the artist. She sat still smiling and getting even more conscious of the crowd. The old man worked with concentration oblivious to the presence of so many people around or perhaps aware but not reacting to it. It takes only one man staring intently to start a crowd in India, the presence of a young Caucasian woman only made it easier. It was a dynamic crowd which meant there were some who would stay for a while, make their wishes, and move on. While there were those who would stay right till the end of the ceremony. And others more who were going about their business but got curious by the crowd and would stop to take a closer look only to go away murmuring half disappointingly, "just a sketch", yet turning around to take a look a couple of times before moving too far away.

The minds of 99% of Indians have not yet been decolonized, a deep-rooted awe of the Caucasian lingers still. Indians tend to put them all on a higher pedestal, irrespective of their education or economical condition. Blacks and even the mongoloid don't receive the same favourable treatment, and in fact are even looked down upon or made fun of by some.

It was considerably hot in the afternoon, yet people lingered around to watch till the end. There was a jubilant roar and applause as the sketch was finished. Kabir paid the artist who quietly charged more than normal. Lucia was too embarrassed to check out the sketch with everyone around and she quickly rolled it up, without looking at it properly. The crowd dispersed as they saw Kabir walking off with Lucia, drawing stares from several of the young men in the crowd. A couple of them commented in Hindi about Kabir being a lucky guy. Kabir heard it and smiled. Having a foreigner woman in your company was looked at enviously in India and was certainly a jump in social status. But he was more amused by the sketch the old man had made. He had been watching it the whole time from beginning to end and he could not hold it any longer. He had to laugh it out.

Fifty Six

"AT LEAST HAVE a look at the sketch!"

"Yeah, but let's first get away from all the people!"

"Hurry up then!"

"Okay... hold on... Heyyyyy! This doesn't look like me!" Lucia exclaimed unrolling the sketch; it was nothing short of a caricature.

"You think so? Well I thought he captured the eyes rather well!" Kabir broke into a laugh, his eyes crinkling with mirth.

"Aaaiii! All this while I was sitting in the heat!" Lucia was slightly disappointed, but she had to admit it was a funny cartoon of her.

"And he was asking for a thousand bucks for it!" Kabir added gleefully.

"What are you saying? And you paid him?" Lucia sounded astounded.

"Sometimes you don't have a choice, but I would have paid more had I known it would be so much fun watching you unfold it!" Kabir kept teasing Lucia, who finally couldn't help but find it funny herself.

"Well he did capture the eyes well..." said Lucia.

"Come let's have a cup of chai? You like chai?" asked Kabir. He would never admit it, but he was addicted to chai as are the majority of Indians, though they too would hardly ever admit it themselves. Chai is the unofficial national drink of India. And the roadside tea stalls are popular with people from all strata of the society. Lucia could do with chai. She had grown to like it and figured that almost everywhere in India there was a slight variation to it. Although she did prefer hers with way less sugar.

Lucia did more of the talking as they both had a cup of chai. Kabir had two cups as he explained that the glasses here were much smaller than in the North and one cup is like half a cup.

"Why is it called 'cutting chai'? What's cutting?"

"Cutting is like half, but you get a little more than just the half. Back in time, there were a lot of mills here and a lot of workers in the mills who lived on daily wages. And to save on the money they would have half cup of chai in their breaks."

"You know a lot about your city or in fact your country..." Lucia pursed her lips.

"Shouldn't I?" Kabir shrugged his shoulder.

"No, I mean it's a good thing."

"Come, we are going to the museum now. We can test how much I know?" Kabir smirked.

Fifty Seven

"HEY, YOU NEVER told me how you felt when you first landed in India. That must have been something, huh?"

"Oh, it was certainly something! I can tell you that. It's like the moment I got out of the airport. It was this heat, WHAM! Like a slap in your face... You know what I mean?" Lucia spoke with a certain gusto that took Kabir by surprise, almost as if she had to get it out. There was this boundless reserve of energy which mostly came out in her art or when she dances. Rarely could one see those bits and pieces of those elements slipping in conversation and rarer still when she was with new people.

"No, I don't know but please tell me." Kabir said with a grin.

"Okay, I'm telling you. So there's this heat already that has just insulated my brain from thinking anything else and then, I came out and there are all these black and brown people with big eyes, and so much noise. It was... ugh... I was a bit scared!"

"Hey, now that's a bit racist!" Kabir laughed at her description which he could well imagine. He noticed when Lucia was excited about something she made a lot of animated gestures to communicate, almost like her whole body was speaking. And she created sound effects that came naturally and might have seemed odd or funny to someone, but Kabir just found it cute. So there was this one side to Lucia which was all poise and solemnly graceful juxtaposed with this other part of her which was like an excited child. At moments such as this her energy pulled at Kabir with a force that filled up all his senses.

"Oh no, it's not racist, I'm telling you what it is. And that day then I wasn't sure I would be able to live here for a month. But it got better every day... better at handling the people... the heat... even the bargaining with cabbies!" Lucia said with a triumphant smile. She recalled all those days that had gone by in such a fury. It was a long time back, it was the first time she had come to India. And then her mind drifted to the first time she came to Mumbai and her smile faded. A thought took her away from herself. She lost her beauty.

Kabir wondered what had made her go quiet, why she looked different, where was she now and whether he should ask her or speak to her. But the eloquent silence told him not to speak but just watch. So he just watched her, he watched her until he was only watching her, he watched her until she came back to herself, he watched her until he could see the beauty regain its colour, he watched her until Lucia became aware of him watching her.

Silence is alive. Its transient, changing from moment to moment. Silence fills itself with calm, tension, expectation, beauty, and so many other things. Everyone perceives it in a way that's best for them at that time. Both Kabir and Lucia were familiar with the power of silence. They allowed it to nurse them.

Fifty Eight

THE CHATTRAPATI SHIVAJI museum was formerly known as the Prince of Wales Museum. Fortunately or unfortunately, the change in name has not had any impact on either the museum or its age old collection.

The impressive black stone building from the British era continues to stand majestic with its huge set of lawns thriving with trees, flowers, and the lush grass. The contrasting black with different shades of green felt soothing to the eyes and the spirit alike. It was a mental relief to find an open space in one of the busiest parts of Mumbai, where every inch of space had been consumed by commerce. But it was a pity that most of this green was inaccessible to the general public. The entry into lawns was prohibited and so was walking on the grass.

A curving drive formed a semi-circle starting at the huge iron gate leading to the porte cochère, which was at the midpoint and curved from there towards another gate. One gate had been given the responsibilities for both entry and exit, while the other gate stood forlorn and bored like some distant cousin whom nobody notices. It was to make it easier for security arrangements.

Along either side of that drive magnificent palm trees stood tall and noble like a royal guard. There were some benches too along the periphery, which could be used for sitting but rarely did someone sit on them. And even if somebody did, the security guards were quick to shoo them off. And the curved road would only see vehicles if a VIP were visiting. Ironically, no Indian VIP was interested in visiting a museum in India unless it was to inaugurate something.

A couple of gardeners were tending the flowering plants and shrubs in the lawns. At infrequent intervals, one of them would pick up the watering hose from a spot and lay it somewhere else. They were only the ones who had the privilege of walking on the grass. But they didn't qualify to be called VIPs.

Fifty Nine

BORED SECURITY GUARDS were quick to stop any curious tourist straying from the designated way, which was to take a left off the curved path after entering from the gate. Then enter the pavilion, buy a ticket from the counter, and pass through the security check. One would next cross a narrow pathway made of stone and join back the curved road a little way ahead. It is at this moment that a little time may be spared to talk about this curious creature of civilization, called the security guard.

Security guards with constipated expressions often tend to be bad tempered and only respond to a display of power. Either that, which is rare, or they are likely to display power which is often. Though, to be fair, this behaviour is not typical to them and can be found in many other people. It is simply more observable in people in a uniform and perhaps more excusable in them too, because of the illusion of distance a uniform creates. Kabir had a theory for it. He thought a uniform causes selective amnesia in people who wear them and demarcates a visible separation which makes people think that these personnel are not like them, thereby, excusing a behaviour of unsolicited authority.

Both Lucia and Kabir had similar strategy towards the security guard and VIPs and that was to ignore them.

"Where are you off to?" A security guard called out from behind them in an officious tone and the same constipated expression.

On most days, any tone of authority made Kabir irascible but today it didn't matter. Today he could afford to ignore it and continued to walk onward. Lucia, who had stopped and turned to look back, noticed Kabir paying no heed and followed suit herself.

"No entry that side. Ticket is this side!" The same voice spoke, somewhat indignantly, unused to being ignored. He pursued after them until he saw Kabir stop in front of a huge yellow sign board, beyond it was an area cordoned off by a thick chain.

This board listed the rules, and ticket prices, which were priced at ten times for foreigners. Incidentally, there was nothing mentioned about not walking on the grass.

Sixty

"WHAT'S THIS! THIS difference in ticket price for the foreigners... It's... it's ridiculous!"

"Yeah, I'm sorry but it is like that," said Kabir impishly.

"Yeah, this is too much of a difference. It was the same at the Taj Mahal also."

Kabir found it unfair to charge foreigners so much more, but he couldn't really do anything about that just then. And such helplessness often knocks on the door of humour to make the circumstances more palatable.

"Yeah, I think our government thinks you guys are rich!"

"Oh, yes, yes... Absolutely." Lucia threw her arms in the air, rather animatedly.

"You guys are rich, and we have to take the money from you. The dollar and the euro..."

"Oh yeah! Well, tell your government not all foreigners are rich."

"Only if government listened to people like me! Come on lets go. The ticket is on me."

"No. I'll buy the ticket. I'm a foreigner, and you are forgetting that I'm rich," Lucia laughed. She didn't let

Kabir pay for her ticket. Ever since the age of 18 she had been financially independent. She felt awkward somebody paying for her. Even on the dates she would usually chip in her half of the money. In fact, even when she was living-in with her boyfriend, she made sure that they spent equally. But that was a long time ago.

Right now she watched how Kabir joked with the ticket clerk that Lucia was an Indian, only a much fairer Indian. He was always good at picking up the nuances of social interactions and had an effect on people. They relaxed and would often smile in this Kabir experience. Lucia felt it was his superpower.

"He thinks you are too fair to be an Indian. I don't think he believed me completely. But do you know there are certain people in India who believe strongly that Jesus was an Indian?" Kabir winked at Lucia who smiled back.

Sixty One

LUCIA LIKED THIS sudden change in atmosphere, the absence of traffic noise felt good to the ears, just as the green was a soothing balm for the eyes.

"It's a nice place to sit and read." Lucia murmured.

"Yeah… you are right. I didn't think about it quite like that…"

Again they passed through the security check where the bags were scanned, and bodies frisked. The inside of the museum was noisier than the driveway outside. The high ceilings made the smallest of sounds echo. And Indians tend to be louder like most of the south Asian communities. Kabir had a theory for it too. He thought the Indians were louder because it was too hot in India. In fact any of the places where the temperature is high people tend to be loud and voluble. And if it's too cold they tend to be quieter and talk less. And that's why the Russian novelists wrote such fat books because they talk less.

It was an impressive monument on the outside, but the interiors were so basic that it gave the impression of a repository of sorts, unlike the palace museums which had ornate walls and doorways with plush carpets. Lucia found this museum to be a little similar to one of those castles converted into museums.

There were three floors and each floor branched out into three or four sections. She loved museums and she could spend a lot of time there, but today she felt relieved it wasn't a huge museum which meant they wouldn't be late for her flight.

Sixty Two

THEY STARTED AT the Oriental section where there were a lot of pottery artifacts from ancient China. The beautiful aesthetics and intricate designs preserved over so many years seemed rather impressive. Kabir couldn't be called a museum person, but he did enjoy reading history. It was his first time at the museum in Mumbai. He was floating from one cabinet to another, humming a tune under his breath. He felt a dip in his enthusiasm feeling a bit left out on losing Lucia's attention to these old artifacts.

"Do you like museums?" Kabir spoke from afar, an attempt at getting back her attention.

"I love museums!" Lucia exclaimed without looking at him. She was looking at an ancient tea pot from the Ming dynasty. Tea drinking was a popular tradition involving a lot of subtlety.

"Really?" Kabir was a bit surprised at the vigour with which Lucia spoke. He walked up to her.

"Yeah, I feel they remind us how we too are here just for a short period of time." Lucia looked up at him. Her large, expressive eyes looked straight at him, casually making their way into his heart.

"We're here for a very short time..." Kabir's throat went dry, and it hit him like a thousand tonnes that she was going to go in just a couple of hours.

"Look at this... how beautiful it looks!" Lucia broke away from the gaze.

"Would you like to have a cup of tea and travel into Ming dynasty, my dear?" Kabir did his version of the British accent, which was rather good.

"Oh, most certainly! Would there be muffins?" Lucia did her own version of it.

They both laughed and for a moment they again forgot about time.

"Come here." Lucia found the strap of Kabir's knapsack on the shoulder was twisted. She fixed it.

"Thanks. So what have you thought of postponing your flight?"

"Well, I don't know, I'm still waiting for the unforgettable experience..."

"Hmm... I don't know, what else to do... I brought you here, took you to the art gallery, to India Gate... I don't know what else." Kabir said throwing his hands up as they both exited that section.

Kabir was tired and it hit him suddenly how stupid he was to think she would postpone the flight for him. There was the obvious question of the fare, of course, and then there was, the major reason, that he was just a stranger to her. What was he even thinking! He smacked his head for even bringing it up. As he dragged himself up the stairs he felt the weight of the impending farewell. This day had been nothing short of a dream. And now he was waking up painfully, wishing he could back to it. Fewer things weigh heavy than an unfinished dream. He was feeling bummed out with life in general now, melancholy tones playing on a loop in his head, beating against the left corners of his chest, and pinching near the armpit just when he would drift back into the dream.

"Kabir, you know what your problem is, you are a dreamer, but in life THEY say you have to be practical, too." A lot of people in a lot of different ways had learnt this phrase by heart and recited it to him. His family, his parents, his cousins, his ex, well, almost everybody had made "They" popular. It always pinched him to hear that, but it was never enough to break his dream. This time it was his own voice he heard saying the same phrase.

Sixty Three

LUCIA SAW KABIR appeared a bit tired. Perhaps he was irritated, she thought, sensing the ripples caused by the inaudible tones playing behind Kabir's inner wall. He was really trying to give her a good day and it felt to be nice in the company of someone who made her smile. But she couldn't just change her plans. Even this roaming around with a stranger like that was just too crazy for her. She had flown on winds of promises only to crash in doldrums. The memory of a distant past now inhibited her spirits like a safety mechanism. But she wanted to give something, do something for him. And then from somewhere a fresh breeze fluttered her wings and she remembered the joy hidden underneath the memory.

"Kabir... Kabir... Wait!" Lucia rushed towards him with fresh energy.

"What?"

"Listen!" Lucia overtook him and stood in front of Kabir.

"What?"

"I have an idea. Why don't you give me your phone... I want to record something on it for you... Which you can only see when I'm gone... And you can do on mine if you like?"

Kabir looked at her for a second. He could see she was making an effort to cheer him up. She didn't really have to but here she was. He felt cheered and relented, pretending to be aloof.

"Okay... We can do that..."

"Sooo you wanna give me your phone?" Lucia took her phone out and handed it to him.

"Yeah... Thank you very much!" Kabir's tone mocked her, wondering immediately after why he couldn't say it with a straight face.

"Okay! Just didn't seem sure a second back!" Lucia smiled coyly.

Kabir felt a bit stupid at this display of emotion, but it didn't take long for the engaging conversationalist to be back and replace the over-thinker.

Sixty Four

THEY CROSSED THE ancient weapons and armours section, passing it with the interest of the pacifist. Then they entered a place where on display were many royal dresses and jewellery of the erstwhile kings and queens. Lucia had seen elaborate dresses in fort museums of Rajasthan. She had been fascinated by the colourful dresses worn by the women, with the brocade and tiny mirrors woven into dresses. It was a whole new spectrum of lifestyle and enriched with such bright colours. Lucia had a strong association with bright colours. She would often use them in her paintings too, as they made her happy. This was also one of the reasons why she loved Van Gogh so much, for the way he used vibrant colours. There were many miniature paintings on display as well, which were a speciality of India. They generally represented a two dimensional view, with a good use of geometry and wide range of colours.

Also on display in the museum was a scene recreated from the past. Behind a glass case a male mannequin was seated, dressed in royal *sherwani*, offering a flower to a female mannequin sitting in her *ghagra-lehnga,* her hand reaching out for it. The depiction read from the royal life of an Indian prince and princess. Lucia had asked about the class distinction that existed in India. She had read about the different castes and had found it rather baffling. Kabir ended up describing in detail how the *brahmins* had established their supremacy by keeping education only to themselves. They had kept the *kshatriyas,* the warrior class, at the second level because they were warriors and could pose a threat. And they had given the third rank to the *vaishyas,* the traders, because they kept the gears of commerce oiled and could also become powerful as they dealt with money. The *shudras, the* untouchables, were the lowest in the order and were no less than slaves, mandated to do all the menial tasks, servants decreed so by Fate. This class distinction was so strong that the lower castes were even denied to drink from the same well. It was the most unfortunate thing ever to happen to India. Kabir himself came from the warrior class called the Rajputs. The Rajput were famed for their bravery and courage. It might have been true then, but he found these claims in today's times irrelevant and baseless. He was just against the exploitation of one man by another.

Kabir explained how cleverly the *brahmins* had used past life karma to exploit the *shudras* in brainwashing them to believe that they deserved their fate. This mental subjugation had made sure that there was never a revolution. Kabir spoke passionately about things that affected him and Lucia listened intently when he did.

"I believe in past life and karma but to use it to exploit and subjugate people is despicable."

"Wow... It's incredible what one human can do to another human."

They were in front of the glass case and Lucia was enamoured of the heavy set of jewellery. She sat down to look closer.

"Do you believe in past life?", Kabir was inquisitive.

"I don't know... But I know that I would have liked to be a Rajput princess in some past life."

"Really? A Rajput princess? Why?"

"Why? Have you seen their dresses and jewellery. I would just love to go round and round and dance wearing one of those dresses!" Lucia remembered watching those gypsy women dance.

"You mean that dress?"

"No... Even heavier than that!" Saying that, Lucia quickly moved out onto the display of miniature paintings. The paintings were displayed at a slant on a shelf that went along the periphery of the room. Lucia had to bend forward to read the descriptions.

"Hey, what's this... Restless Majnu... What is a 'Majnu'?" she asked, looking up from the painting as Kabir shook with laughter.

"Not 'what'! *Who* is *Majnu*!"

"Ohh... so *who* is *Majnu*?"

"*Majnu is*... So you know Romeo and Juliet, right?"

"Yes."

"Great. So here we have Laila and Majnu... and Majnu is the Romeo... that's why he is restless..." Kabir said and moved forward unaware of the little joke the Gods were playing with him.

"Restless *Majnu*..." Lucia repeated. As she saw Kabir walking ahead she couldn't help but smile.

Sixty Five

THERE WERE SOME interesting sections in the museum, some more than the others. Like the one they just saw, then there were some boring sections that showcased old utensils used which they quickly crossed. One can't help but wonder at these vain extravagances that humans indulged. There were a lot of Indian mythology on display in the paintings on fabric which caught their eyes. Lucia found these two dimensional art form interesting. Unlike the west, where renaissance had introduced innovations like realism and then later the progressive forms of impressionist art. In India, the paintings didn't evolve much and was mostly two dimensional. And then there is a particular section devoted to Buddha and Buddhism. As they entered the hall they were greeted by a smiling golden Buddha statue in the centre with various intricate paintings around it depicting the tales from the Buddha's life.

"So did you go on a spiritual journey in India?" Kabir asked.

"You could do well as a professional guide..."

"Yeah, I think so too... So, did you?"

Lucia didn't know how to answer his question. It had definitely been life transforming for her. She had come here looking for love and had ended up discovering that perhaps she didn't understand love. So maybe in a way that could be called spiritual. She weighed her words as she thought of this transformation that she had undergone and simply said,

"Yeah, I guess so... But isn't that a part of being in India?"

"I suppose it is... We are the best market for spirituality. But jokes apart, did you go to some meditation centre or yoga ashram?"

"No, not really. But I guess I discovered something peaceful, hard to put into words."

"Maybe you can paint it?"

"Yeah, maybe I will!"

Lucia smiled for a long time. There was this void that she had felt, and she truly believed that someday, someone, would fill that. Maybe it had to do with having her family split at an early age. And it's this that led her from one failed relationship to another, leaving her disappointed. But it's a common mistake most commit, wanting to fill an inner void with something from the outside. She loved India for many things and one of them was to see how successful this concept of joint families was in India, where people were not isolated and were there for each other. The void was still there but she had learned to accept it and not chastise it, at least on the surface. Little did she know that this calm on the surface can sometimes hide whirlpools and undercurrents that lay deep within.

"You know, these are for sending out prayers. You rotate them clockwise." Kabir walked over to the Buddhist prayer cylinders strung in a row on one side of the hall. He rotated them as he made his way forward murmuring his prayers. Kabir was deeply spiritual and was happy in this space. Life had taught him many things, most of all that no matter how much we surround ourselves with people, but at the end we are all alone.

Lucia followed suit and spun them as she wondered where and to whom these prayers were going.

"You know what it says?"

"Nope..."

"*Om mani padme hum*. It means inside me is a lotus and inside the lotus there is nothing..." Kabir had asked this of a man who once had lived as a monk. A monk who had become his friend.

"That's beautiful!" Lucia repeated the prayer in her heart. It reassured her. And a glow emanated in her eyes which was coming from her heart. Kabir looked at her eyes, and she looked at his. He was smiling. She was smiling. The whirlpools stopped momentarily, to catch their breath.

Sixty Six

SOME PEOPLE FIND museums boring, what they don't understand is that museums are not meant to entertain, they are here to ease the pain of aging.

The museum moments had been cathartic, letting them shed a bit of their baggage on the platforms of the past, to accept their temporal nature. They walked out of the museum on to the VIP driveway, their feet cushioned by a shared comfort. The palm trees guards leaned towards each other, whispering a breezy welcome to the two old souls enriched by their shared experiences.

The craving minds and souls might have been soothed with the relics of the past, but their tummies growled for food. And instinctively people look at their watches when they feel hungry. Kabir too looked at his watch. It was 3 o'clock. But there was no reason to be anxious, the engineer in him had it all calculated. They were doing good on time. They could catch a quick snack at Victoria terminus. An hour then to reach Simi's place and half an hour from there to the airport. So they would easily be there an hour and half before the flight. Kabir did the quick mental math as

Lucia said something about Indian food, which escaped his attention. He had a habit of getting late, due to a callous attitude towards procedural work and also because his math was always based on the best case scenario or rather the overtly optimistic case scenario. Fortunately or unfortunately, life has a different definition of the best case path. Today, under the weight of responsibility, Kabir's math was taking into account the obstacles that might come along the way. But even so old habits have a way of reinforcing themselves through surprising new ways and means. Not everything can be planned for.

As they were walking out towards the taxi stand, they came across a flute seller playing a flute. A middle aged man with dark eyes and combed hair sat next to a tree on a stool next to a *paan* shop. He had a big conical basket that had flutes growing out of it like petals of a flower. The man was breathing out a beautiful tune, an age old *raga*, perfected by time and filled the empty spaces of the afternoon. It formed a bridge that stopped people from falling into the abyss of siesta. Lucia stopped near the flute seller, transfixed by the melody. She liked the melancholy sound, and instinctively held Kabir's arm to stop him, but didn't let go of it until the song was over.

Sixty Seven

"THIS IS ONE of the best things I like about India, every place has its own sound. You know what I mean?"

"Yeah, I know what you mean..." Kabir was a musician himself and he was quite familiar with the different kinds of music and instruments that existed in India. Although there was a lot of western influence in the songs he wrote, he was equally attracted to the Indian classical and folk music. And he liked to infuse Indian instruments, especially the tabla, into his music.

"I feel very refreshed after hearing the music, Kabir..."

"There's a reason behind it. That tune is in a raga apt for the afternoon. It's called *Bhimpalashi*, it soothes and refreshes. Different ragas have different effect on the mind, and they have their own times in the day... and night."

"I wanna hear more... But can we eat something too?"

"Yeah... Let's go to a place I've in mind for you. I really like it." Kabir checked his watch for time and hailed a cab. He held Lucia's hand and with his other hand signalled the oncoming traffic, navigating to the taxi in midst of the rush.

"VT, dada," Kabir said to the driver as he scooted in.

"People are quick to honk here!" Lucia rushed in behind Kabir who had got in with surprising deftness. Lucia realised how Mumbai could suddenly put pace into things. A minute back it felt they had all the time in the world and now they felt an urgency even about breathing. She could hear sounds the *damru*. This was the *damru* that was making the world dance. It didn't take them long to reach VT. The sound of the *damru* would take a while to settle down.

"This door on my side won't open. Do you mind?" Kabir gestured to Lucia to open the door on her side as he quickly got his change back from the driver. Some taxis in Mumbai have their right side door sealed shut. It's a bit of a safety mechanism so that people don't get down into the side of oncoming traffic.

"We've reached already?" Lucia got down quickly as Kabir slid out right behind her. Just in nick of time the traffic restarted.

"Look there..." Kabir loved the view of the Victoria Terminus. It stood grand and if you looked at it long enough you were bound to travel through time.

"Yeah, some traffic!" Lucia could never get used to looking at this sea of humanity and traffic. Her heart was beating to the sounds of the *damru*. It was overwhelming for her with all the honking. She just wanted to catch her breath.

"No, not the traffic. Up there..." Kabir turned Lucia towards VT.

"Oh, wow, that looks amazing!" Lucia was reminded of some of the magnificent buildings of Europe.

"It's a UNESCO world heritage site, right there..." Kabir said proudly. The late afternoon sun put a golden glow on the buildings to last till the early evening, before the dusk would make it look orange and then later at night the different coloured lights, put up strategically, would look rather splendid. As they stood on the side, regaining their lost breath, they gazed in wonder at the huge building that made all the traffic and everything around it look so small. Lucia took out her phone and took a couple of photos.

"We can go closer..." Lucia was glad she didn't miss this by going to the airport early.

"Yeah, but let's grab a bite first. You are hungry, right? Let's cross." Kabir pulled at Lucia's hand and in the next moment she found herself being pulled across the road. 'Let's cross' was not a question, it was a command. The roads were busy all the time at this junction, and there was no foot-over bridge and neither an underpass. Crossing roads in Mumbai at such junctions was quite a risky task. When they were across Kabir gave a triumphant smile while Lucia's face expression read *Don't ever do that again!* For the briefest moment all the sounds had ceased and then they came rushing back at a gallop.

Sixty Eight

"THAT WAS CRAZY!" Lucia said, her breath caught midway.

"Have you had a vada-pav?" Kabir grinned.

"What?"

"It's an Indian burger, famous in Mumbai. And these guys give you one of the best vada-pav." Kabir and Lucia stood next to a counter which was serving takeaway vada-pavs; it was an extension of the restaurant next door.

There was a constant flow of people coming in and out. Plus they had a counter outside where a few people in their maroon uniforms were working like a machine. With the number of people who were coming and going, it must be really good, presumed Lucia.

There was a cashier handling money and announcing the orders smartly, and there were two workers making the vada-pav by putting some green and red chutney between buns and inserting a ball of mashed potato in-between before handing it over wrapped in a piece of newspaper sheet. All this was happening like clockwork.

"So, I'm gonna order two normal ones." Kabir told Lucia as he approached the cashier holding out the money in his hand. Lucia discovered this early on that people didn't really follow a queue in India and it was mostly about who could reach farther and first or who could draw the attention to themselves. There was always this rush for things, and she wondered why.

"Two vada-pavs, one less spicy, and a bottle of water."

"So vada-pav is like a potato patty of sorts with a bun. And of course, some chutney and masala in it." Kabir explained as he returned after placing his order. Lucia saw some people were taking their orders to-go. And the man who was wrapping was doing it in a unique fashion and with metronomic regularity. As soon as the vada-pav was slid his way, he would quickly wrap it up in a piece of newspaper sheet and tie it up using a thread drawn from a spindle hanging overhead. He would then call out the order when it was done.

"So, here you go!" Kabir brought their orders of vada-pav.

"How do you eat it?" Lucia asked as she held the vada-pav with both hands in a paper plate. It looked too big to take a bite from. The potato patty was not a patty but a sphere!

"Okay, so you just press and flatten the *vada* by pressing the bun. And then you try to take bite without making it spill. Don't watch me while eating!" Kabir stuffed his mouth with a big bite and looked away. He chewed through the smile and awkwardness of Lucia staring at him studiously as did all the people around. That included the people working at the counter, other customers, the bystanders and the even some of the passers-by.

They were more interested in watching Lucia eat their favourite delicacy. It gives almost all Indians a strange sense of pleasure when a foreigner takes up to their food or clothes or language. Perhaps it acts as a bit of validation and also the warm feeling generated by the dwindling separation between the two cultures. And there were some definite signs of triumph in the crowd expressed in the form of nods and smiles, as Lucia managed to take her first bite of the vada-pav.

"How's it?" Kabir asked chewing through the remnants of his previous bite.

Lucia felt the initial softness of the pav and then the crisp fried *vada* breaking through with the amalgamation of spices and potato, taking over her taste buds. It was steaming hot and a bit too spicy. But she liked the overall taste and texture, though she found it a bit dry. She gestured an A-Okay sign to Kabir as her approval of the dish. It was something very Indian to do. Much to her surprise and Kabir's amusement, she got an A-Okay sign from the waiters and other people around. Kabir's mouth was too full to laugh, and they were all passing nods and smiles to each other along with light murmurs. They had a story to tell back home today.

Of course there were other Indians who stopped to check what was the whole commotion about and some would mutter, "just a foreigner eating *vada-pav*" and go about their business. But there were also others who suddenly felt an impulse to have a *vada-pav* themselves.

Sixty Nine

KABIR HAD TWO of those while Lucia felt one was heavy enough. After completing their meal and giving ample material for stories to the people, they left there and walked closer towards the statue of Feroz Shah Mehta. It was in front of the Municipal corporation of Mumbai building. Next to it, a platform of sorts had been erected where people could stand and admire the architecture and also think on how they couldn't go inside. This building along with the Victoria Terminus comprised the heritage site. Only a small section of the terminus was accessible to the general public, the portion that was connected to the platforms. The other major part housed the office of the Railways. Kabir explained how the statue of Queen Victoria used to be there under the canopy under the clock tower. It has been missing and untraced, most likely sold by the politicians. And people mistake the statue on top—the symbol of progress—to be the statue of Queen Victoria.

There were some other tourists as well who were clicking photos on the platform. Kabir and Lucia took some photos too. It gave time for the body to adjust to the food. Food too has effects of slowing down time. The vada-pav had made their movements a bit sluggish. And then they just sat down on the stairs opposite the statue of Feroz Shah Mehta.

"Kabir, who is that?" Lucia asked reading the caption of the statue.

"Oh, he is Feroz Shah Mehta, a great Indian lawyer." Kabir explained about Feroz Shah and his exploits in the British courts. He emphasized proudly how he had won against the British in their own courts. He talked about how the British had marginalized and belittled Indians in that era and to stand up against the might of that empire was very heroic. Kabir felt Indians today lacked a national character and he explained how they are not really ready to fight for their rights. In fact, they don't care for their rights, they are puppets in the hand of politicians who influence them and divide them on the basis of religion, caste, or anything else that worked for that moment. Lucia listened intently and liked Kabir's passion for things. Sometimes she felt she could relate to them and sometimes she learned something new.

"This area reminds me of being in Europe. The architecture and the structure."

"Yeah, it does look like that."

"I like European architecture, and art..."

"You do? Which painters?"

"I like Van Gogh, Picasso... In fact, if I could paint like Picasso, I'd paint you..." Kabir looked straight into Lucia's eyes as he said that. And unknowing and unforeseen forces beyond his control had begun to paint her. We all paint an image of people we interact with all the time. Most images tend to be what we perceive which may or may not be how those people visualize themselves. In that moment Lucia felt he was painting an image agreeable to how she saw herself.

"Oh, come on, so what Picasso painting you like?" Lucia blushed and using extreme powers of concentration caught herself from flowing in the moment. And instead, she thought about Cubism for the bit.

"I saw Guernica, which was pretty good…" Stark images formed a mural over the sky with skewed shapes and faces emoting the torment and Kabir's eyes went to the horse neighing over humanity like dark clouds of the inevitability of war and strife that hang over humanity.

"Yeah, that's a good one… you know what's it about?" Lucia felt the air around her grow heavy and it was not just the pollution.

"Yeah, it's about the Spanish civil war."

"Very good. It is about the Spanish civil war and actually, in particular, about air bombing of the town of Guernica by Franco." Lucia added to the canvas from her imagination using the stories she had heard mostly from her grandparents. The tales of the macabre survive through generations to teach their lessons. Lucia wondered what the people of Guernica had done to deserve to be bombed by their own countrymen. The conflict between the Catalans and the Spaniards was on at that time.

Lucia spoke about her country with a passion that reflected how much she cared. She talked of how her people were divided between Catalonia and Spain and there are many who would like to be separated. She thought how everywhere people were separated.

And today it occurred to her how easy it is for people to find ways to create separation between each other. In that light she saw Kabir to be someone who bridged the gap with his words. Perhaps it was the legacy of his name.

They both were silent for a while. The noise outside didn't matter because the noise inside had ceased.

Seventy

SOON ENOUGH THE lights came up on the buildings in front of them and it was like magic. As if the universe had intervened to make the mood lighter. They sparkled for a while, catching Lucia and Kabir's attention and they were off. Perhaps it was an hourly thing, Kabir wondered as he hadn't seen the lights come up like that before sundown. They were the only tourists sitting there and it was like having their own private show. Meanwhile, Kabir had booked a cab to take them onwards.

Kabir got up and again held Lucia's hand as they crossed the busy junction hopping and running to get into the cab waiting for them. The day was done and Kabir had run out of ideas. There wasn't much left to be done except to drop her off at the airport. It had only been a few hours yet there had grown between them an intimacy which was surprisingly deep. No stranger could have guessed they had just met that morning. Lucia had a smile in her eyes that came out of feeling relaxed. She was at ease in Kabir's presence and intrigued by his ideas. She now just had a long wait at the airport before reaching home. So many days she had spent in India and everyday full of surprises, but this day had been something else altogether. Her waned energy had been rejuvenated.

Kabir spoke to the driver as was his habit to engage in talks with anybody and everybody.

"Where are you from, brother?"

"UP... Benaras." The driver was a balding man in his late 40s, sporting a thin twirling moustache. He spoke in clean, confident voice and an amiable tone.

"Oh, what are you saying, buddy! I love the city of Benaras!" Kabir exclaimed joyfully. Incidentally, the Saint Kabir was also born in Benaras. It is said that those who die in Benaras go to heaven and every year you have thousands who turn to the city of Kashi in their old age for their salvation. But the Saint Kabir chose to die outside Benaras because he wanted his karma to decide what he deserved.

"He is from Benaras." Kabir turned to look at Lucia and tell her as she watched this spectacle of Kabir working his magic on people yet again.

"You didn't tell me your name?"

"Ram Plate Yadav," answered the pleased cabbie. It was a unique name and Kabir asked him twice if he really had heard the word Plate in the name.

"Oh, what are you saying! You have become our charioteer then!" Kabir spoke referring to Lord Krishna who drove the chariot of Arjuna in the great battle of Mahabharata. Krishna too was from the Yadav clan. The driver understood the reference and had a beaming smile now.

Seventy One

LUCIA HAD OBSERVED many times during the day that Kabir had a way with people, He made them feel important and was genuinely interested in hearing what the other person wanted to say. But it was the first time she wondered at what point he had worked his magic over her.

"So Yadavji, it's like this... I have shown madame various places in Mumbai today, but she just didn't get impressed... So take us somewhere... somewhere... that impresses her completely."

The bemused driver thought for a bit, tapping a finger on the steering wheel. Then he said, "Hmm... *Yes, there's one place... Foreigners really like it... I'll take you right away... And it's on the way, too!*"

"*So hurry up because time is in short!*" Kabir checked his watch they were skirting at the edge of 'no time'. He wondered what place this driver had in mind which he didn't know of himself.

"*Of course, sir, on the way we... You tension no take !*",

"I'm just telling him we are short on time," Kabir told Lucia who was looking out the window.

"Yeah, I know. *Hurryingly take us, brother!*" Lucia jerked herself forward in the seat as she spoke and went back again. She had spoken in the Bhojpuri dialect of Hindi spoken in parts of UP, leaving Kabir baffled. He couldn't believe Lucia had said that. He thought his mind was playing tricks, but he had undeniably heard her speak!

"What! *You...* You..." Kabir was stammering for words, shocked out of his wits.

"Look at your face!" Lucia laughed. She hadn't planned on telling him earlier, but then decided why not on the spur of the moment. Lucia had picked up Hindi pretty quickly and it was important for her too, as she was studying classical Indian dance forms. Many a times she had pulled off this trick where she would not tell people present that she understood Hindi, silently observing what people said letting them believe she didn't understand. Yes, the different dialects and accents could be tricky, but she would still get the gist of it if she concentrated hard enough. But never had it been so satisfying as today.

"Oh my God, you speak Hindi?" Kabir looked bewildered. His pitch had become sharper, and his tempo was faster owing to the mixture of anxiety and excitement. Excitement because a foreigner was speaking Hindi and anxiety because he had no idea what all he had said through the day thinking she wouldn't understand.

"No, it's Bhojpuri, actually." Lucia pointed out with her finger, correcting Kabir with an innocent and angelic expression.

"Oh my God. So you understand Hindi?" Switching to Hindi, he asked, "*You are understanding this as well? Whatever I'm saying right now?*" He spoke the Hindi at bit of a slower pace, treading these unknown waters with measured steps, to fathom the depths of his confusion.

"*Yes... Little, little I understand...*" Lucia replied back. She was having so much fun.

"I don't know even remember what all I've said through the day!" Kabir wondered out aloud.

"Ahh, yes, but I do!"

"That's so not fair though!" Kabir retorted.

"*Just a little joke I played on you...*" Lucia spoke in chaste Hindi.

"Wow... *Little joke...*" Kabir was both impressed by Lucia's Hindi and the fact that she sounded very cute saying those words in her own unique accent. He couldn't help breaking into a grin, amused by the prank that had just been played on him. But he had turned red when as he remembered all those moments through when he had spoken in Hindi. He had passed quite a few flirtatious comments.

Lucia had been rather amused by Kabir and his friend Simi as they had discussed her. Or on those occasions when Kabir spoke with the waiters or at other general moments. The way Kabir would speak to people who were considered to be of lower social status, was something she had been impressed with. It was in fact the major reason that had impressed Lucia about him.

"*Brother, full day she didn't tell me that she understands Hindi so well!*" Kabir shared with the driver, overwhelmed by this sudden turn of events.

"Sir, Hindi talk aside, she's fluent in Bhojpuri!" Ram Plate Yadav was equally impressed hearing the white lady speak in his native dialect. He had heard foreigners speak in Hindi but never Bhojpuri.

"It was just a small joke, brother." Lucia smiled shyly like a small child who had been caught doing mischief.

"Little joke... Baaprebaap!"

There was an atmosphere of jest, of the belongingness of old friends sharing new stories after a long hiatus, starting their conversation from where they had left off.

"My God, I have no idea what more secrets you are hiding!" Kabir thought of a lot of things. He wondered what Lucia's story was. He wondered what had made her come to Mumbai and most of all how would he explain the goof-ups of the restless *Majnu*!

"No, no more secrets for now." Lucia had a twinkle in her eyes that wasn't the reflection of the setting sun.

"What! You see me... how I'm sitting now?", Kabir crossed his arms, pointed to his closed body.

"Are you hiding something?"

"No, I'm not hiding, I'm protecting. You are the one hiding secrets... Are you?" Kabir added the last bit rather impishly which was unintended.

"No... Okay... Yes, but I will tell you later."

"You are something!"

Kabir was smiling. Lucia was smiling. They were smiling together.

Seventy Two

A NEW DIMENSION had opened up between Kabir and Lucia. It was not just about the attraction between two people of the opposite sex anymore and was more than the intellectual admiration they had formed for each other. The seed of friendship was germinating, allowing in them both the ability to feel vulnerable in each other's presence. It is perhaps the most compelling ground of compassion and mutual respect that allows such a bond to form. But its seed has to be sown first and that initiation had been done. Time would do the rest. And Ram Plate Yadav, the driver, was the lucky spectator to watch it in its nascent stage and would end up providing a reason to laugh together.

Lucia had had no plans on disclosing to Kabir that she understood Hindi. It gave her the feeling of having an edge and also offered her a sense of protection against the unknown. Now even though Kabir came across as a decent, well-mannered person, you can only know so much about strange men in distant lands in so less a time. The duration of time needed has been proverbial since time immemorial in determining how much we know a person, even though it's the nature of circumstances that really reveal the truth about a person. And here too it was finally the circumstances that had made her drop her guard, in what can only be termed an organic manner. Lucia, after acting on an impulse, wondered whether she should have told him this sooner, was he offended? But she had more pressing things to ponder over like how she felt a bit vulnerable with exciting thoughts about Kabir whizzing through her mind bombing her brain with endorphins and dopamine. All of it had the effect of dilating her pupils and making her feel more alive, scraping off some layers of hurt she carried that Kabir had no idea about.

Kabir's initial shock made way for embarrassment as realization struck like lightning. 'Lucia had understood every word he had said' percolated from his ears into his mind and settled in his heart letting the butterflies flutter in his tummy. And for a while those butterflies flew in brilliant colours only visible as a blush on his cheeks. They settled down on the colourful flowers that bloomed in his heart, only when it dawned on him that Lucia was still there with him and that, certainly, had to mean something good! The butterflies would remain on those flowers and watch the entire show.

Kabir felt a little vulnerable knowing that Lucia knew how he felt about her and that he was attracted to her. What must have she thought of him? Oh! How foolish could he have been? And various other such embarrassing questions had the butterflies flutter the moment they were beginning to settle down. It made him feel more alive, almost effervescent.

Meanwhile Ram Plate Yadav, oblivious to the endorphins and butterflies, had been charioteering like Krishna on the battlefield, unaffected by internal dilemmas. The taxi came to a halt near a bridge and Kabir wondered where they had reached.

"*Sir, we have reached,*" Ram Plate Yadav announced proudly.

"*Yeah, but we are where?*" asked Kabir.

"*Dhobi Ghat. Foreigners this place very much love and come here for photos,*" replied Ram Plate.

"*Dhobi Ghat* is a place where the washermen come and wash the clothes. But you know what *dhobi ghat* is, right?" Kabir blew out the butterflies with a sigh, realizing he needed to stop translating for Lucia now. And oblivious to him, the butterflies flew, spreading the pollen everywhere in him and more flowers were to bloom.

"No, not really. I don't know everything in Hindi," Lucia admitted sheepishly.

"Ah! Well, it's a place where washermen come to wash clothes."

"*Yes sir, do check it out. Madame will love it!*" Ram Plate spoke with rare confidence.

Kabir and Lucia crossed the road over to see some clothes drying.

"Hey, look, some foreigners!" Lucia exclaimed.

"And now you are officially an Indian!" quipped Kabir.

"Well, he was right about the foreigners clicking photos," Lucia added coolly.

"I had got my hopes up on the unforgettable experience..."

And they both burst out laughing, thinking of the confidence with which the driver had told them about the place.

"Unforgettable experience it is!" Kabir took a snapshot of Lucia, and they went back to the cab.

"Kabir, can we watch the sunset somewhere? I wanna look at a sunset in Mumbai "

"Sure, we can, from..." Kabir's voice trailed off as his mind went into a time equation. He checked his watch: they did have half an hour to spare at best as it was going to be a bit of a rush after that. The damru played its beat and Kabir could hear it. It would keeping playing in the background for this one last time.

Kabir loved watching sunsets and it was something he wanted to on his last day in Mumbai. After all, he was leaving the city for good that night and might not be able to come near the ocean for a while. Lucia had him forget all about it and now she was also the one to remind him of it. Kabir had a notion that was also his reply to the question of 'beaches or mountains'. Sunrise in the mountains and sunsets at the beach.

Seventy Three

HUMANS SWARM TOWARDS water just as moths swarm to the light and in similar numbers. There were quite a few beaches in Mumbai, nothing unusual considering the long coastline that the city had. Mumbai may be imagined in the shape of a tall, lean person laying north to south along the coast, with an ever increasing, protruding belly, that stretched out from east to west. There were many areas along the coast that had no beach but had been cemented to form a promenade with lifeless wave breakers that looked alive during high tides. It allowed the large population of Mumbai an easy access to the sea.

There was the Worli sea-face and then there was the Bandstand or the Carter Road in Bandra. But the most popular of them all has to be Marine Drive, fit to be a queen's necklace, and quite rightly called so. It offered a great view during the day, but its true beauty could be seen at night when the whole promenade shone like many stars lit up forming an ethereal necklace adorning the goddess of sea. It attracted a wide range of people in large numbers every day. From your fitness enthusiasts formed by joggers with their hi-tech watches, earphones, and FitBits, and the surprisingly fast paced older men and women who moved in groups mostly, uninterested in gadgets but not lacking in spirit. Then there were the loners who would sit pensive, arousing curiosity in anybody who looked at them. Some others came for a 'me' time after getting off from work, and some others still came in search of the meaning of life. Then there were the many lovebirds with colourful feathers but black and white lives, surpassed only by the cars in numbers. Excellent at finding nooks and crannies, this species never fails to make you gasp 'now where did they come from?' when they transpire out of the thin air. Their families living in tiny homes offered zero privacy just as narrow mindsets allowed zero space for their love for any manoeuvring.

A country that had produced the *Kamasutra,* was ironically rather tough on the public display of affection.

Seventy Four

KABIR AND LUCIA found a comfortable spot. Both of them were silent and restfully so. The sounds of the waves had drowned the distant sounds of *damru* for the time being. But if you have heard a *damru* play, you would know that it beats at a steady rhythm and then there is a crescendo that breaks the character, much like the waves of a sea that go back and forth steadily and then a big wave comes that catches you by surprise.

The Arabian Sea paints a quiet and gentle picture unlike the torrid temper of the Bay of Bengal on the east coast. Many fisherman boats could be seen floating lazily in the distant horizon. They would be back in a couple of days to their wives who would undertake the task of selling the fresh pomfret while the amphibious husbands would fill themselves up on coloured waters of the land before venturing out to the sea once more.

It had been a long day and physically tiring, too. Looking at the sun slowly making its way into the sea felt rejuvenating. Sunsets have a hypnotic effect on humans not unlike how lamps hypnotise moths. The only difference being that while the sodium bulbs act as weapons of mass destruction on unaware insects, the sunset heals, applying a balm of peace.

Kabir, like many Mumbaikars, had come on several occasions and shared his inner most feelings with the sea. Mumbai and the sea formed a pair much like the yin and yang. In a city that could entrance you with its dreams and make you forget things in its haste, the sea was a patient listener, always offering itself to anyone and everyone. People emptied their hearts out into the sea with what they had filled it in the city. Perhaps to that effect, the city allowed the people to be like rivers, forever flowing, carrying along debris dumped in them, and forever growing. Unfortunately, a lot of the city's literal waste was also being emptied here into these waters that once upon a time might have been blue.

Lucia, used to gazing at the cool blue waters of the Mediterranean sea under the deep blue sky, found the colour of the sky and water here different because of the pollution. And even though the sky and the water seemed strange, yet they gave her that familiar sense of comfort, speaking to her in that same language that her heart understood. The sun rays were still reaching out to her just as in Barcelona.

Seventy Five

LUCIA LOOKED AT Kabir who was looking intently at the sea with a gaze sprang from the well of gratitude. He was very relaxed,. It had been a long time since he had spent a day like this. Ever since he had moved to Mumbai, he had been just too busy chasing a dream. A person used to working at a job with fixed working hours didn't realise here too he had to take breaks. It's a big shift to become a freelancer. You are now the boss as well as the employee. The boss is always demanding, and the employee never learns to take mind off work. So even if he was not writing or composing, his mind was still switched on as he was looking for work, which is the major preoccupation of a new artist. And now to have to drop it all and go back was difficult. Lucia was not a just a woman to him. She was like... She was... He couldn't find the right words, but he was thankful.

"I feel the sun and the sea are two lovers and that the sunset is their union. How the sun's rays reflect over the waters like a lover caresses his love, teasing with his fingers, and every passing moment brings them closer to each other.

The sun flaunts and parades its myriad hues across the sky, while the sea gradually, effortlessly, pulls the sun towards itself until finally enveloping it into a tight embrace."

By now Lucia knew Kabir was a charmer with his words but that didn't stop her from feeling goosebumps when he spoke in that voice reverberating through the chest, the voice of a heart that's beating strong and gentle.

"Do you like sunsets?" Kabir asked, looking at Lucia who was gazing at the sea.

"I love sunsets. I can paint them as many times as I feel the urge. You know what I love best... how the sun's rays keep coming to me all the time...it makes me feel special..." Lucia smiled. She had loved this ever since she was a little girl. Whenever she stood in front of the sun she could go back in time to when she was just a 4-year old visiting their beach house along with her family. It was her first memory of the sea. And her mother had told her how the sun was coming to her. She saw the sun's rays reflecting on water making their way straight to her. It had made her less afraid of the waves that had looked huge.

"But you are special .." Kabir mumbled

"What did you say...?" Lucia asked, pulled back from her reverie.

"Nothing .. I said I think the sun is like a seasoned performer..."

"Sun is a performer?"

"Yeah, a thorough professional that comes every day with the same act but always does a new trick at the end to take everyone by surprise."

Lucia looked at Kabir and smiled thinking how she could have kissed him. She wanted to kiss him, but no, she shouldn't. Gentle waves of emotion tugging the heart, on the shores of love.

"We gotta go, else we won't make it on time." Kabir pushed himself out of the trance to get up. It was the sudden crescendo of the *damru* that graciously played its part.

"Let's sit for just a little longer, no?" Lucia wasn't yet ready to break away her glance at the sun.

"No chance... I don't wanna take a risk with the traffic!" Kabir was getting a bit anxious.

"Oh, come on, five minutes won't be a problem!" Lucia said pulling Kabir down. He sat down reluctantly, overpowered by the gentle persuasion but his mind was not there. It was everywhere, in a *tandav* of thoughts in sync with the beats of the *damru*. Every wave was the big wave now. If it were his flight he wouldn't have been that anxious, but it was about somebody he didn't know too well yet cared for deeply. People react differently in stressful conditions, and he had no idea how Lucia would be if she were stressed. Moreover, he would feel terribly guilty of having her miss her flight. Avoid unnecessary stress whenever possible was one of the things that he had learned, and that honesty was the only way out.

"Look, I'm really getting stressed. I don't want you to miss your flight..." Kabir said in all sincerity. There was visible anxiety as his left foot kept tapping.

"Okay, don't be stressed... My flight has been postponed." Lucia spoke in a matter of fact tone. She took hold of his arm and pulled him closer. Kabir wasn't sure what he heard. It was an abrupt stop to the thought that stood midway in its one-legged tandav position, eliciting a dramatic beat from the *damru* as it too scratched its head with one end of the thread.

Seventy Six

"YOU WHAT?"

"I postponed my flight."

"No way!"

"Yeah, I did, too!"

"What? When?"

"Can we enjoy the sunset?"

The sky had turned as crimson red as Kabir's face and the reason in both cases wasn't entirely different. Lucia took hold of his arm and rested her head against his shoulder. Kabir's mind was surprisingly blank. The thoughts that had been called out for *tandav* and the *damru* both made an unceremonious exit from the stage. The curtains had been drawn and light instrumental music played in the background as the audience held its collective breath in suspense of what was to come next. On the exterior it reflected as a smile around the corner of his lips, joy in eyes, and a marked disbelief on his face, uttered as a question more to himself than to Lucia.

"What about the unforgettable experience?"

"Watching the sunset together is quite unforgettable, don't you think?" Lucia cooed. She was relishing the effect the news had had on Kabir who could have been in a lucid dream for all he knew. But it was not him alone who was affected. She felt a strong rush inside her and like the undercurrents that run beneath the surface of the sea invisible to the naked eye, so was her pulse racing. She had never done anything quite like this. She had bought a ticket for this new ride and now she stood there in the queue for what was about to come. What if he was just joking? Would she have enough time to board her flight? She would also have to pay the airlines an extra 50 euros although that was the smallest factor. And all sorts of factors had gone into the reward to risk analysis that she did. The ratio was small but that was because both the reward and risk were high. The heart rarely bothers for calculations and the head too relents to the matters of heart. Now, while she stood in front of the rollercoaster with a thousand questions dancing in her lit mind, as if to answer all her questions Kabir spoke again,

"I remember these lines by Kahlil Gibran.

'How often have you sailed into my dreams,

And now you come into my awakening,

Which is my deeper dream.'"

Poetry puts us at ease, perhaps only because it doesn't merely put to rest the questions of the intellect but assuages the torrents of the heart that give birth to those questions. For Lucia it was like finding a friend who stood in the same queue and now she had someone to share the ride with.

Seventy Seven

"YOU KNOW, ONE of my favourite poet is Rumi." Kabir's heart was rushing. People make wishes, they don't expect them to come true. And that's why they don't know what to do when those wishes do come true. Kabir was that person right now. And now that it had come true, he didn't know what to do, or to say.

"Rumi... Yeah, I know Rumi... What does he say?" Lucia, flowing with the same current that Kabir was flowing in.

Kabir forgot what lines he was going to quote of Rumi. The moment he looked at Lucia, his mind went *tohu wa bohu*. And when that happens, spontaneity takes over unhindered.

"He said you should find someone to watch sunsets with. I think that's what he meant..." Kabir wondered who was speaking as he reflected on the words he had just uttered.

"You are something..." Lucia gave him a look of disbelief as her face flushed. She rested her head on Kabir's shoulder as the rollercoaster took a sharp right turn. And Kabir's body which had been tensed earlier, relaxed, adjusting itself to Lucia's closeness. And they made a beautiful painting together, as they watched the sun meandering on the surface for a few moments longer before uniting with the sea. The afterglow of the sunset in the Mumbai skies owing to pollution in air creates for a mystical view. Filled with shades of orange and purple that change with every passing second, creating some new visions afresh. So while the sky wears colours that have no name, they also reflect on the sand until it's all dark like the glow on the faces of playful lovers after the union before they restfully sleep.

Seventy Eight

THERE IS A zest to life in Mumbai, and it can be observed more so at night under the stars. No wonder it's called the city that never sleeps. A similar energy was reverberating between Kabir and Lucia that was demanding of them to paint the town with their colours. They wandered until all the shades of orange had turned into all the shades of purple and all the shades of purples had turned into black. They were both more themselves in each other's company now. Kabir seemed less anxious to please and Lucia seemed more open to share. But Kabir seemed listless now, quite literally so, what with all the places ticked and the unforgettable experience achieved. The feelings were much like that of children on their first day of summer vacation. There was no milestone left, and he didn't know what to do. His mind was a tabula rasa. So it was no surprise that Lucia was the one who took in the reins of togetherness in her hand, only to let it gallop.

"Don't you think we should celebrate? I could sure do with a drink..."

"And I know just the place!" Kabir jumped at the opportunity, getting up with a sudden burst of energy.

"As long as you don't make me walk…"

"Of course I'm gonna make you walk!"

They had bidden the taxi goodbye. They were young, the night was young, and waiting for theirs to be. And just how a few extra hours of togetherness could have such a big impact on each other's lives, is what they were soon to find out.

Seventy Nine

THE TRAFFIC WAS louder, the lights looked brighter, and it seemed all of Mumbai was out on the streets. People eating street food savouries, eyes dripping with tears of joy in spices, women in groups walking with their shopping bags stopping and bargaining with shopkeepers who stood out of their brightly lit shops, clueless men picking out vegetables slower than the children licking the ice cream running down their arms, some bored tagging along hearing but not listening, clued-in men steering wonderstruck women, teenage girls trying out accessories taking selfies in the street shops, teenage boys acting cool and taking selfies in front of them, vegetables vendors and street hawkers announcing loudly over them all. The youngsters zipping past on their scooter and bikes with blaring horns looking for attention, the occasional beggar pestering for attention, the little kids tugging at sleeves demanding attention, and old men sitting idly and chatting, done with attention.

To an outsider it could seem like some festivities were underway, but that's how it was every evening. It was the nature of the streets common to an Indian city.

Lucia always felt enchanted by the many colours in such proximity and wondered whether Indians looked happier because of this caravan of colours or was it because they were happy and expressed it with colours. As she observed loud excited groups of families all together out shopping, she strongly felt that nobody could feel lonely in a place like India. But just as the mirage that appears from afar is unobservable from near, so was this fete of colours. An illusion that hid the little intricacies and dynamics of society, making everything look beautiful but a closer look would disclose the poor, the impoverished, the exploited and the depressed.

Kabir, much too used to the atmosphere, steered Lucia gently like an experienced captain at the helm of a new ship.

Eighty

"HEY, LOOK AT this." Lucia stopped at a shop with a lot of glitter that made her eyes go all wide open. Artificial gold and silver jewellery shone under a simple bulb giving the effect of a cluster of stars brought together. These were ornaments mostly made out of metal and given a brass, silver, oxidized silver, or a golden finish, with artificial gems of different colours. She held a heavy and intricately designed earring that looked like the spread out feathers of a peacock. She put it on her ear as Kabir stood looking at her, smiling, thinking how women all around the world love glittery things.

"Do you wanna buy?" Kabir thought they looked pretty on her.

"Yeah, but I'm afraid they are too heavy for my ear." Lucia quickly put them back lest she be tempted. The shopkeeper was quick to take notice of her.

"No, madame, it's very light. See. This hangs like here and comfortable." The shopkeeper was certainly very enterprising as he himself wore the earring within seconds and explained to her how the string behind it distributed the weight evenly. Lucia was both surprised and a bit amused. Most of these street shop were nothing more than a cabinet opening out, with small incandescent bulbs hanging over them, creating a brilliant light effect, making the glittery things all the shinier, the shiny even more glittery, having an almost hypnotic effect on women of all ages and even some men too.

"No, thank you," said Lucia with a smile. She wasn't sure whether she would be able to wear it in Spain and that was her rational part taking over.

"See something else, madame. Give you special price!" The vendor wouldn't let go of a customer too easily. Most of the men in India don't express their feminine side which every man has. But salesmen in clothes shops or jewellery shops in India couldn't care less and often put the sarees or the uncut cloth piece against themselves and pose, even sway the clothes for the women to have a better idea of how it would look on them.

When Kabir saw the man putting on the earring he was instantly reminded of a similar incident from his childhood. He had gone out shopping with his mother and the salesman had posed in the same manner. He felt a pang of nostalgia which only momentarily reflected on his face. It had been a long time he had spent time with his mother.

Lucia brought him back to the present and he was smiling again.

Eighty One

"I LIKE THIS jhumka or jhumki... What do you call this?" Lucia said playing with the little bells that hung, tapping them with her finger.

Many days later Kabir would be able to put into words what he had found most endearing about Lucia was that in a moment she could transform into a little child and then back again into a lady.

"Okay, you know stuff..." Kabir smiled.

"Of course, I'm a woman!" Lucia said pragmatically.

"So, well, in Hindi generally when something is big, it's given a male gender and if its small it's given female gender like..." Kabir broke off as a strange thought struck him. Could someone think of this as gender biasing in culture? He had come across women who he viewed to be on the sharper pitch of feminism and could take everything under the sun as a gender bias. The thought dissipated just as fast as it had risen by what Lucia said next.

"Like matka, matki... " Lucia looked up from the jewellery with a bright smile.

"Yes, very good..." Kabir grinned, impressed by her quick reply. He found Lucia's accent of Hindi rather delightful. He remembered when he was rehearsing for an English gig, his friend had told him to try to form words in the front of the mouth. Most of the European languages including English are spoken at the front of the mouth. The languages of the subcontinent are spoken with the words forming at the back of the mouth. So that's why when most foreigners or the NRIs speak Hindi, they speak it like they would speak English. Knowing all of that didn't stop Kabir from feeling Lucia's accent any less cute.

"Let's go," Lucia said as she quickly walked ahead using a surge of will to pull herself away from the stall.

"Madame! Wait! Special discount!" The salesman called out behind her while Kabir shook his head for a no.

"Don't want it, brother!" Lucia shouted back in Hindi, astounding the shopkeeper as much as Kabir who gave a 'you heard it' look at the vendor.

Kabir caught up with Lucia who had stopped at a stall selling necklaces.

"That looks pretty." Kabir winked at Lucia in the mirror coming from behind as she was trying out a necklace.

"Yeah, it does... doesn't it?" Lucia had a long neck particularly suitable for the heavily ornate necklace that she was trying on.

"Do you want it? How much?" Kabir asked the seller in Hindi. He wanted to get her something but wasn't sure how she would react to it. There was still a culture gap he felt, making him hesitate about giving gifts.

"No, I don't want it. *Chalo*!" Lucia was now comfortable peppering some Hindi words along the way.

It was a narrow pathway along the main road with stalls on one side showcasing varied things ranging from sunglasses to first copy or second copy watches, perfumes, handicrafts from different parts of India. Shops ranging from big brands of footwear, watches, small fashion boutiques, even some restaurants and fast food joints were strung out on the opposite side. Between them there was a constant rush of people trickling either way, all setting their own pace. Most of the women (some of the men, too) walked as if hypnotized, gazing intently with open eyes from one stall to another while their men protectively steered them through the oncoming pedestrian traffic to keep moving. Kabir followed suit as he too took a position behind Lucia with his arms around her whenever there was rush, ensuring nobody touched her inappropriately. Yes that could happen perhaps more in other cities, but Kabir was not taking any chances in a crowd. On the lighter side Kabir noticed Lucia was drawing envious stares even from some of the fellow females on account of two reasons – because the women got less attention at the stalls where Lucia would stop. And because the men accompanying the women would steal glances at Lucia too.

Eighty Two

"I FEEL LIKE buying them..." Lucia admitted wistfully.

"Ohh... do you wanna try them?" Kabir teasingly held out a beautiful pair of earrings that looked like the sun with rainbow colours, tempting Lucia.

"Do you wanna try them?" Lucia walked ahead, not turning around. She knew they were tempting her.

"Well, do you know I did have earrings back in the day? When I was in college..."

"Really... That's interesting."

"Yeah, and I had long hair... I was in this whole rock zone." Kabir spoke with a sudden zest that can only come from remembering one's college days.

"Yay!" Lucia made devil horns with her fingers and banged her head in air.

"Yeah, exactly. Can you do that again?"

"You mean this..." and then Lucia did her little devil head banging.

"You are so cool! I wish I had met you before!"

"Of course you wish!" She grinned devilishly.

"I'm glad that you postponed your flight..."

"So am I."

Lucia's hand found Kabir's as they navigated their way through the crowd. For a while they both forgot about time and everything else.

"Did you buy gifts for your family?"

"You mean souvenirs?"

"Yes."

"Why do you think the bag is so heavy?" Lucia winked at Kabir. She went onto explain all the things that she had bought for her mother, her grandmother, her cousins, her friends, her aunt. She had a big family, but rarely were they all together. As she told Kabir about the things she bought in different towns of India, she thought about the feelings she went through at those points in her journey. It had been very haphazard, and she had just gone with the flow.

Lucia had been forced to contemplate looking at the joint families in the Indian small towns and villages, on how it must be living with all the family under one roof. That would truly be a home, a familiar sense of belonging. Her parents had separated when she was very young. And it always made her feel incomplete, going from one house to another. When dad was there mom was not and when mom was there dad was not; she was deprived of them being together for her. Perhaps that's why she was always on the lookout for someone to make a home with. India had become a teacher for her. What was about it, she couldn't put it in words, perhaps she could have described using colours. And this painting was still taking shape in her heart. So many new colours had been added in one day.

Lucia felt Kabir's hand gripping her a little tighter as they came at a junction to cross the road and entered a club. It was a lounge with a dance floor and from the happy faces of people there it looked like a fun place to be. Kabir hoped Lucia would like it. He didn't know what she liked so he had picked a place that he liked himself, which had been the code of the day.

Eighty Three

"I LIKE THE music."

"Great. I'm gonna have a beer. What are you having?"

"Beer works for me…" Lucia's foot was tapping as she grooved to the music. The music soon took over her body as Kabir watched with delight.

Kabir paid for the two beers upfront at the bar before Lucia could even launch a protest.

It was dimly lit but not so dim that you couldn't see anyone's face. There were small yellow lights that sprouted from the ceiling hither and thither. There was a place to sit outdoors, and there was a dance floor inside. Maybe we could even dance for a bit, she thought to herself.

"The next round is on me!" She took hold of her bottle.

"We'll see about that. First tell me how do you say cheers in Spanish?"

"Cheers! Oh, Salut!" Lucia liked that word and she loved saying it.

"Salut?" Kabir was quick to pick up the tonality and the accent. If he could hear it he could repeat it.

"Yeah… Salut!" Lucia gave an approving look with her eyebrows.

"Okay, Salut!" Kabir looked thrilled and they hadn't even had a sip.

"Salut. Okay now we drink!" Lucia laughed at the *saluts* flowing unhindered.

It was the first of many salutations for the evening.

Eighty Four

"DO YOU PLAY that?" asked Lucia pointing to the foosball table as they both walked away from the bar.

"Sure, we can play. You know how to?" Kabir asked. He loved to play foosball and he considered himself good at it.

"Yeah, but I'm not so good at it," Lucia admitted.

"Alright then, Spain vs India! In real football we wouldn't stand a chance against your team. But today we have!" Kabir couldn't have been farther from truth.

"Oh, yeah, we do have a good team. But not so much football here?" Lucia asked casually.

"No... We mostly play cricket." Kabir tossed the little white ball onto the foosball table and the game was on.

And before long Kabir was getting his ass beaten by Lucia in the game.

"Hey, I thought you were not good at it?" Kabir laughed as Lucia scored another goal to bring the score line to 7-1.

"Well, I guess I just played against better players. Plus, I'm Spanish, football is in our blood..." Lucia shrugged her shoulders, teasing Kabir with her tongue out.

Lucia could be competitive and wasn't going to make it easy for Kabir who had thought he could take it easy on her since she said she wasn't that great a player. But it didn't take him long to realize that she was out of his league in football. So what if he was not good at foosball he still had the gift of gab.

Eighty Five

"HEY, SO YOU never told me... what made you come to India?"

"Well, actually... Umm... I had come down to meet somebody but... It doesn't matter." Lucia shook her head more to herself than for Kabir. She wanted to talk to someone about it but then it had been such a good day, she didn't want to ruin the mood. Plus it's hard to put in words things that you are overwhelmed with. Little did she realize that her mood was already off. It was just under the surface, and she had avoided dwelling on it and thanks to Kabir, she had even forgotten all about it. Now it was just upsetting for her to be reminded of it again.

Lucia had gotten deathly quiet and Kabir didn't know whether to prod her or not. She hadn't looked so serious before. Her moves in the game became more aggressive leaving her defence vulnerable and Kabir was quick to score a goal.

"Goal! Goal! Goal!" Kabir imitated the Spanish commentators.

"Very good," Lucia was amused by Kabir's little victory dance. She was still in the lead but not for long.

"So no ballet boy waiting for you in Barcelona?"

"Nopes... well, actually, I had hopes with this guy here... But it wasn't supposed to be..." Lucia spoke dejectedly. Her face seemed calm, but her aggression was felt by the foosball table as she hit the player rods. Even a cave man could have understood that this woman was angry. And Kabir was a pretty sensitised man and rather intuitive.

"What happened... Do you wanna talk about it?" Kabir remembered reading 'a good listener can solve anything'. It was time to try it out. It's strange in a funny sort of way to watch how the brain assimilates all sorts of information when it's really set on achieving something.

Lucia clicked her tongue as she bent down to collect the ball out of her corner. It was another goal scored by Kabir. Lucia had a temper, but she rarely let it out, sometimes if she got really very angry she would just cry. Some people hurt others in their anger while some people just hurt themselves. Lucia was the latter and had it not been for her dance she would not have been the good natured person she was. After all a person can only take so much pain and not be damaged. She wasn't always like that, but she had been disappointed by so many and hurt so much that it had taken a toll on her. Being inexpressive about it didn't help either, as it would stay inside her to come out in something else. Fortunately, she had always loved to dance and that gave her a way to exercise it all out that would be just boiling inside her.

Kabir was a conversationalist of the highest order with a constant need to keep it engaging and it's something that also allowed him to form new relations. But it was his often underestimated and under-appreciated ability to stay quiet at the right times that made him good at keeping those relations alive.

As is often the case in matters of the heart, once stirred, it wouldn't take long for Lucia to speak up again.

Eighty Six

"SOMETIMES YOU INVEST so much in a person, and it doesn't amount to anything. I hate that feeling. I came here all the way from Barcelona, and he is here with..." Lucia was angry alright, but she hadn't lost her poise then and she wouldn't lose it now.

"...with someone else. That must have made you really angry." Kabir completed the sentence.

"You think so! I could have hit him!" Lucia hissed vehemently the last part barely audible, but Kabir caught that.

"Wow! I can't believe you really hit him!" Kabir, caught there by surprise, spoke triumphantly as if saying serves him right.

"No, no, no... I wouldn't do that!" Lucia became embarrassed at her little outburst, what she had said was not what she meant. After all, she wasn't really the sort of a person who could hit anybody. But then again, most people think that about themselves until they have been brought into a situation where they are truly tested. And only a strong belief and self-control can stop them from being violent in those moments. Luckily for Lucia, the discipline of a dancer and the patience of a painter ran deep in her. She had seen violence at a young age and that's why she despised it. But a lot of people never want to act in the manner they despise but invariably do. And when Kabir voiced her words, she realized the gravity and it subdued the violence inside her. But there was a conflict within her. She was torn between what she wanted to do and what was the right thing to do. In essence that's what anger tests.

Kabir studied her silence, her body moving in anger, her words talked of self-restraint while her eyes nursed a hurt.

"So this guy is in Mumbai?" Kabir spoke with a seriousness, a tone of his unfamiliar to Lucia until now.

Lucia simply nodded avoiding eye contact to stray off the conversation. As she ran her fingers through her hair pulling them back on all one side while inside her head, several thoughts from all directions collided against each other, adjusting into a single file of questions. She was lamenting now, why did she have to mention it in the first place? What was she even thinking? They were having such a good time, but it was too late now. Too late because Kabir was in no mood to drop it.

"Give me his number. Now!" Kabir had a grave expression, the usual glint of smile in his eyes replaced by a steely gaze, accentuated by the bridge of tension formed by the coming together of his brows.

"What! No, why?" Lucia asked, shocked.

"No, give me his number right now."

"Why do you want it?"

"No questions! Just give me his number... You don't have to worry..." Kabir looked aggressive, and Lucia finally came out of her stupor as it struck her why he was asking for the number.

"No, I don't want any trouble Kabir... Let's just forget it!"

"No, he is not gonna get away with this... I'm gonna call him right NOW!" Kabir was bristling and Lucia stood a bit surprised to see Kabir in this avatar.

"I'm gonna go to his place... and I'M GONNA TELL HIM TO HIS FACE... Thank you!" Kabir spoke raising his voice almost to a shout and then bringing it down ever so deftly at the point of uttering 'Thank you'. For a minute, Lucia didn't know what to say in this rush of emotions. What did she just hear him say? Was it some kind of a joke? What just happened here? Again thoughts collided causing a flux of neurotransmitters in her brain. She heard Kabir continue speaking.

Eighty Seven

"WHAT?" SHE COULD articulate only that one word.

"Thank you! Yeah... I'm gonna thank him. Thank you so much... Because of you I met the most amazing woman in the world!" Kabir's tone back to his usual cheery self, only if it could be called usual for the effect it created on Lucia was nothing short of spectacular. As the drama came to a climactic close, it broke off some chains of resentment that held at Lucia's spirit, and the heart was racing, her mouth agape partly for a loss of words and partly for want of more oxygen as her brain rewired. For the untrained eye, the effect showed in the form of a smile but for the trained eye, it was visible everywhere. A weight dropped off her shoulders and her body adjusted to this newfound lightness which no amount of alcohol could have brought. The crux of this day percolated through her mind as a single concentrated thought that everything happens for the best.

Lucia didn't know what to say as she looked at Kabir who stood with that big grin and the glint of smile back in his eyes knowing fully what he had achieved. A new chain of thought sprouted in her mind that such an event is quite like the miracle of watching a seed germinate grow or a flower blooming. A single thought has the power to change perspectives. And Lucia romanticized life as she wondered whether she went through all that just so she could meet Kabir or was it that Kabir came into her life so that she could feel this way. It was not over yet.

"You are the most amazing woman I have met Lucia. I'm so glad that I got this day with you." Kabir spoke looking right into her eyes. The words were redundant here as his eyes conveyed it all. He had been blown away by Lucia and finally he had said it. Ironically, it was she who was blown by him now.

Lucia wanted to say something back, but she let her body do the talking. She stood there with a wide grin, her hands resting on the table as her body leaned towards Kabir. Her neck at an angle with her hair falling all on one side. She tried to look away, she couldn't. Meanwhile, Kabir, with a swift motion of his hand, rolled the rod and it hit the ball, a lucky shot that scored.

"India! India! India! India!" Kabir shouted with a little victory dance.

"India indeed..." Lucia murmured though it was not all for that winning goal.

The scores were equal, and the beer was over too.

"I think we should grab more beer. Plus I don't wanna lose the game from here!" Kabir said.

"Alright... Fair enough..." Lucia's smile just wouldn't dim.

By taking Lucia on this joy ride of emotions in this dramatic fashion, Kabir had managed to help her see things in a different light. We often get to hear things happen for the best or whatever happened was for the greater good and a part of us wants to believe it too, but it's mostly intellectual gibberish. Until the good becomes visible as an experience do we truly know that whatever happened, had happened for the best. Kabir had provided Lucia with that gratification. True, she had come to explore India and to understand herself better on this solo trip. But to be acknowledged and appreciated by another human being moves us all profoundly. The essence to be loved and cherished is perhaps the most basic need. Kabir hadn't planned on behaving in any specific way or that it would have such an effect on Lucia, he had just done what felt right to him. He had improvised in the moment and those words had come to him.

There was a bounce in Lucia's step now.

Eighty Eight

"YOU KNOW, I had no idea and that it would be such a fulfilling day." Lucia spoke loudly over the music. Formality slipped into words to compensate for the inhibitions they had shed.

"Well, I'm glad I got to spend all this time with you." Kabir saw Lucia looking towards the glass door and then she kept her beer at the ledge and darted off towards it. Someone was entering from other side though it was too dark to notice from where Kabir stood.

"CARLAA!" Lucia screamed at a tall foreigner with curly hair, who shrieked as excitedly noticing Lucia. And they were excitedly hugging, jumping, and talking in Spanish, nineteen to the dozen. After a while, quietening down somewhat, Lucia brought Carla over to the table where she and Kabir were standing.

"Kabir, I want you to meet Carla, Carla this is Kabir!" Lucia was electrified.

"Nice to meet you, Carla." Kabir put out his hand with a smile.

"Nice to meet you, too." Carla shook his hand politely, eyeing him a bit suspiciously and went onto talk animatedly with Lucia.

Kabir felt completely ignored, feeling a bit out of place. For a second or two, he tried to feign interest in their conversation, but he couldn't comprehend what they were saying and slouched back a step or two. He had in an instant lost all of Lucia's attention which had been on him throughout the day. It did him good as it gave him a perspective of reality, things which he had completely lost touch with. Interestingly, that's what Carla gave to Lucia as well, a realistic perspective.

Lucia went onto explain Carla, her hands moving animatedly, how she had met Kabir and how he had shown her around the city. And that she had ended up postponing her return flight.

"Loco!" The first thing that Carla said to that and the only word that Kabir did catch. She thought Lucia was being crazy and told her to be careful and that she is in India. Lucia just nodded in affirmation and said Kabir was a nice guy. Carla retorted nice guy or not, to just be careful. It was good advice on the part of Carla as she was only worried about her friend. It was good he couldn't catch the rest of the conversation it would have certainly made the Majnu restless.

Lucia, realising Kabir was feeling left out, brought him back into the conversation.

"I was just explaining to Carla, how we met and the day we had," Lucia said to Kabir patting his shoulder.

"Yeah, she is a really an amazing person," Kabir said to Carla.

"Yeah, that she is!" Carla gave him a stern smile and again went back to speaking in Spanish telling Lucia to be careful. She gave her number to Lucia before leaving, telling her to call her in case Lucia needed any help before she flew back.

Eighty Nine

"WE HAD MET in Agra, and it was like, how you say, finding someone who speaks your language. So we went to Taj Mahal together and then she was going to Rishikesh, and I went along with them. She was with some friends." Lucia had loved Taj Mahal so much. It had made her cry the first time she saw it.

"She seems like a nice friend to have." Kabir acted cool, sipping through his beer. He had been feeling a bit left out, and he didn't do a good job of hiding it.

"Yeah, she told me to be careful…" Lucia looked at Kabir with a grin.

"I had a feeling she did." Kabir's earlier feelings flew away with a laugh.

"Wanna dance?"

"At your own risk. I'm a terrible dancer!"

"Come on… It will be fun… Just don't step on my feet!"

"No, I'd never do that, but you know when I'm gonna come to Spain and…" Kabir followed Lucia down the stairs.

"You are gonna come to Spain?" Lucia stopped midway, looking back at him.

"Yeah, and I'm gonna learn Spanish, too."

"You are gonna learn Spanish?" Lucia stopped again, turning around.

"Yeah, why not... It's the second most spoken language after all."

"Second or third, I don't know..."

"Yeah, so I'm gonna come to Spain... and learn Spanish. But I'm not gonna tell you I understand Spanish, and I'll have my *Revengo!*"

"You'll have *Revengo*..." Lucia laughed and Kabir joined in as they made their way onto the dance floor. Their imagination was already dancing on a plane where they would float to in a while.

Kabir felt clumsy in front of the graceful Lucia who was like a magnet drawing everyone's attention. Some of it fell on him making him conscious. He knew a few moves that were not easy to do but he was a bit stiff.

"You gotta loosen up to dance!"

"Yeah, well I'm feeling a bit conscious..."

"Don't be. You want I stop looking at you?"

"Never!"

"Show me your moves then."

Lucia was in her element, floating like a butterfly, and sprinkling her glitter on all, while Kabir stood mesmerized under her spell.

The closer Lucia came to him the more relaxed his body felt. She was enveloping him in her air and when she was close enough such that their noses could have poked at each other, they were there but not present. They flew on a magic carpet away to where only their imaginations had reached. Where there was no one else but them and the spirits of heaven that propelled them. For several minutes not a word between them was spoken and the spell that had cast itself continued to be even when they stopped dancing. For there was something about them that drew the eyes around them even as they walked off the dance floor, the magic alive between them.

Ninety

LUCIA AND KABIR were a little drunk but quite in their senses as they made their way back to the waterfront. They were crossing the road when a car zoomed past them dangerously close jumping the red light. Lucia cursed at the driver in Spanish scaring the driver in a parked vehicle nearby, much to Kabir's amusement who broke into his loud laugh.

"What did you say? You scared the shit out of him!"

"He deserved that." Lucia was emphatic.

"Well, I won't argue with that!" Kabir blurted between laughs, still finding it funny.

"Yaar, you always laugh like this, so loud?" Lucia spoke uninhibitedly as she looked at him questioningly, her mouth puckering in a half-smile. She had picked up 'yaar' in the one month here. Kabir stopped laughing, eyes squiggling queryingly.

"I mean don't get me wrong, I like it..." Lucia smiled, she did find Kabir's laughter infectious.

"Well, we are Punjabis. And in Punjab, everything is grand. Everything is larger than life. Like the way we celebrate things. Hence the laughter is loud too. Even in Bollywood films they show a Punjabi wedding because its grandiose and visually appealing," Kabir said, proud of his heritage. And almost as if to make a point he sat with his legs stretched out and his hands behind his back supporting him. He had a pretty good buzz going in his head and it had certainly let his inhibitions down.

Several people earned their livelihood at night from people who had retired after a dog's day. Among the many creatures of the night, one of the most interesting specimen, rather unique to Mumbai, is the masseur offering their services on the Marine Drive. Many such masseurs passed by them as they sat on the pavement, offering different options. As is usual in India where any tradesman calls out what he is selling, so does the masseur.

"Do you want a massage?"

"I won't say no to that".

"Yes, bhaiya, madame wants a massage!" Kabir called to one such masseur.

"Head massage, foot massage, full body massage…" The masseur spoke in a fast mechanical tone.

"No, no, I don't want a full body massage!" Lucia broke into a laugh and shook her head vigorously.

"Foot massage, madame. Good massage!"

"Good massage… *Desi price ya videshi price,* Taj Mahal ki tarah?" Lucia teasingly asked making the masseur smile sheepishly.

"*How much for, bhaiya?*" Kabir asked the price in Hindi.

"Foot massage, 100 rupees. Full body massage. 500."

Lucia and Kabir broke into a laughter again.

"*Nahin, only foot massage.*" Kabir said.

"Pukka good massage?" Lucia asked as she removed her sandals.

"*Ekdum* relax!" The masseur replied confidently and started massaging Lucia's feet. He was carrying a kit with him like the rest of his comrades on a mission to remove stress. This little kit contained some oils, rag cloths, and a few other unrecognisable items. The guy must have been in his early twenties, stockily built, wearing jeans and a shirt. He had a straight posture and spoke confidently.

"What's your name?" Kabir asked the masseur.

"Salman."

"Oh, Salman! You know Salman, he is an actor in Bollywood?"

"Of course I know Salman Khan! How you say, old is gold?" Lucia was enjoying the massage. Her feet had been sore from so much walking and then dancing.

Ninety One

NORMALLY WHEN WE suspect inhibitions, we generally gauge it from the manner a person interacts and never really from the matter about which he or she interacts. Kabir was an extrovert who could talk and engage with anybody in a conversation. Most could never say he had any inhibitions because he hid them well, lying deep within. He would never really express his feelings and had it not been for his songs they would never see the light of day. Perhaps being in a big family, everybody sort of missed out on hearing what he had to say. Either they were too occupied with their own things or just forgot that the then little Kabir too felt something. He saw everyone crying out their own pain and he hesitated burdening them with what he was experiencing, no matter how big or small. Lucia had spent the day observing Kabir and the closer she came, the clearer it became how Kabir used a happy-go-lucky veil to cover his feelings.

"Kabir, why don't you talk about yourself?" Lucia asked in a plain tone. She had been looking out at the sea. The foot massage had come at a good time.

"What do you wanna know?" Kabir asked nonchalantly.

"Well, okay. Tell me why you took this sabbatical and now are going back to your old job?" Lucia didn't understand why someone who knows what they love to do and are good at it would go back to do something they didn't like. Lucia noticed Kabir's shoulder suddenly tensed, and his body became a bit stiff. She was sitting alongside, chin resting on her knee, head inclined to a side waiting for Kabir to answer, who heaved a big sigh before answering.

"You know, it's not easy chasing your dream here. You just can't do what you want to do in life. Like singing is not even considered a proper profession here. So I don't make the decision, my father doesn't take a decision, rather it's his brother doing that. Why should anybody else take a decision for me?" Kabir's despair was evident in his tone.

"And you know, initially they didn't even know I had left the job. And then we stopped talking!" Kabir scoffed.

"Really? You don't talk to your family?" Lucia felt a wave of compassion flowing through her as she listened to him.

"No, we talk... I talk to my mother, but it's not the same thing, you know?" Kabir looked desolate. He had never had any support from his family. And monetary support is helpful but much more than that is the support that comes from the belief that people have in you. When they don't give you that, it leaves you marooned on the island of disappointment. None of them ever truly believed that he could make it and it was difficult to live with that.

"I thought, like, joint families must be good. With so many people who are there with you. And not being ever alone..." Lucia said trying to show the bright side.

"You know, you are lucky, because you guys are free as an individual. Here the individual is not free." Kabir spoke passionately, wishing in that moment to have been born in some first world country. And when he said 'you guys' he meant it collectively, of all the people born in all those countries of the west. Of course, he had no idea about the life and struggles over there. He only had an impression of evolved people and happy spirits. But Lucia had seen individuals on the station of oblivion where the lonesome trains took them to the next stop of isolation, with nobody to give them company on this journey. It was especially more difficult for the old who even lacked the support of work. It was diametrically opposite to living in India where you could never get a moment alone. But she didn't know that people were lonely here even in a crowd.

"But you have people to share responsibilities, who can care for each other!" Lucia saw the utopian side of the families. She didn't know the innate nature of human beings to dominate the other, to control the other, can be more so in families where words like tradition take precedence over choice. And the individual is required to fit themselves into a mould created for them.

"They never care about what I want?" Kabir had the last word. He looked at Lucia as he spoke and then looked away immediately, afraid to show too much emotion. But not before Lucia managed to see the hurt in his eyes. It made him look so vulnerable. She didn't know what to say. It must be difficult to give up on a dream. Her hand instinctively went to his shoulder, and she massaged it tenderly.

"*All okay, it will be...*" Lucia looked at him tenderly as she spoke this typical Hindi phrase used often, no matter how intractable the problem.

Kabir broke into a smile and a little laugh spurted out as he repeated what Lucia just said. Least expecting this to hear from her.

"*All okay, it will be.*" Kabir believed it for a moment when he said it. He found Lucia's accent endearing and her company soothing. Lucia was glad and a bit relieved that Kabir had finally smiled. And not giving him much time to think about the hows and whys, Lucia sprung up with feline agility, lifting the mood with her.

"I wanna have ice cream. Let's have ice cream!"

Ninety Two

PARTLY, IT WAS because she really wanted to have it and partly it was just some quick thinking on her feet to lift the spirits. She remembered how her mum would take her to have an ice cream whenever she was upset. Ice cream just turns a bad day into a good one.

"Let's go. I know just the place!" Kabir gushed instantly. His enthusiasm was back as he thought of the famous Natural ice creams. Kabir thought how he could have forgotten Naturals! Natural's ice cream was a speciality of Mumbai, and everyone swore by it. They had many parlours all over the city and now extended even to other cities. Their ice cream was a mix traditional ice cream and the Indian style kulfi, giving it a homestyle touch and came in various flavours. The seasonal fruit flavours were the more popular ones.

Lucia liked the effect ice cream had on Kabir, she thanked her mum for the idea.

It's the plight of many Indian children that their parents fail to understand them. In India, a deep rooted belief has been strengthened over the years that parents are always right. Perhaps it's because parents have given them birth. In many families even when the children grow up and become parents having children of their own, they continue to focus their time and attention on their own parents. In the worst case scenario the next generation children grow devoid of attention and fail to develop an individual personality of their own. On the other hand some parents give too much attention to their children trying to mould them in the shape they want. If it's not the parents then it's the school, the teachers and the whole system that's bent on conditioning the young minds. Again the children fail to develop their personalities. And the children who do develop a personality can have a hard time adjusting to an insensitive environment and exercising their own free will. Doing what they wish to do in their lives becomes a difficult process for them. Difficult because the very first step of determining what they love to do can only be understood when the external influence stops. Kabir was lucky in the sense that he knew what he loved to do. He was also lucky to have had the courage to pursue what he loved against all odds. He didn't know that yet.

He was also lucky he had come across Lucia today of all the days.

Ninety Three

THE ICE CREAM parlour was brightly lit with posters of ice cream sundaes looking delightfully enticing. It is the one place where everyone becomes a kid, the moment they step through the door. It was pretty much past midnight, but the place was bustling and the only people talking were the ones who didn't have an ice cream in hand. There were those who were silently eating in a corner and then some would go out with their cups and cones. Fastidious customers were trying out all the flavours and were still unable to decide which one to order. Then there were those who would come straight up and shoot a well-rehearsed order for the whole family. Kids changing their minds at the last minute on the flavours they want, the different coloured flavours visible through the glass panels having a hypnotic effect on them.

Kabir and Lucia got a cup each and then found a seat outside. Lucia liked the subtle flavour of custard apple. The ice cream tasted different here in India primarily due to the difference in the taste of milk. Lucia and Kabir grinned at each other like little kids as they relished their ice cream.

The waning effects of alcohol revived by the sugar allowing for conversing on topics which had not been touched upon before. Kabir was only noticing Lucia. Lucia was curious and couldn't hold it any longer as the ice cream came to a finish.

"So what next?" Lucia asked plaintively.

"Nothing, go back to my job." Kabir shrugged as he scraped the last remnants from the side of the cup.

"So you are gonna give up on the dream?"

Kabir stopped midway as his body responded to the uncomfortable question. Giving up is easy to do but hard to admit.

"No, it's not about giving up... I tried... But I guess the world doesn't want any more singers and writers..." Kabir finished the sentence nonchalantly and ate the last bit of his ice cream. Saying it out aloud seemed to give a sense of comfort. He didn't wish to indulge into a deeper thought just then.

"So you are gonna stop singing and writing?" Lucia seemed naively inquisitive, closely reading his body language. Kabir straightened himself up lifting off some weight.

"No... I mean... I don't know. I mean, like as an artist... Who is gonna want to listen to me?" Kabir said with slight discomfort, avoiding eye contact. He tossed his ice cream cup into the bin nearby in frustration.

"Were you singing for yourself or for the rest of the world?" Lucia scraped the last bits of her cup and she sat leaning towards him with all her attention.

"No, I mean every artist is doing it for himself, right... But, sometimes, as an artist, you just need someone who is there to appreciate you and your art. You want someone to listen, read, or watch... and if that's not the case then... what's the..." Kabir broke off midway and went silent. He heaved a big sigh looking out at the horizon. The moon, hidden out in the distance behind a cloud, was motionless and helpless. He took his eyes off it and his shoulders slouched, upset that things hadn't worked out the way he had wanted.

"Yeah, that's true!" Lucia spoke emphatically drawing a faint smile from Kabir.

"Well, if it makes any difference, I'd always like to hear you sing." Lucia looked intently at Kabir, her eyes repeating every word she had just said. And this unexpected attention, care, and love from a person that Kabir had met few only a few hours ago made his throat go dry. He kept looking at her as something inside him felt different. And out in the distance the cloud dispersed, and the moon shone again.

"Thanks," Kabir smiled. It was a feeble smile, but it came from deep within. It was a smile of hope that had braved a storm.

Ninety Four

SOME HURTS DON'T heal in an instant but what matters is the initiation of the process of healing. It had begun in Kabir, and all it took was just one person's attention. Just like Kabir had been the catalyst in Lucia's healing earlier that day, she had now unknowingly returned his kindness in kind.

Kabir took the empty cup from Lucia and disposed of it. She picked his knapsack from the chair and together they walked out holding hands under the sodium lamps of the night. They walked for a while, there wasn't much to say and neither the need. The comfort they brought each other spoke for both of them. The night breeze was cool, filled with sounds from somewhere in the distance, echoing in the air. For a long time they both had not experienced this feeling in anybody's company, where the mind was quiet and the breath deep.

Kabir suggested they take the train, as they were near the train station. The experience of Mumbai can't be complete without the train ride, he explained.

Kabir bought the train tickets and led Lucia to the platform. The train was already there and was ready to depart. Lucia had seen photos of overly crowded trains and people hanging onto the grab handles and was consequently a bit reluctant. But she had Kabir with him who had made the tug of war of thoughts pretty one sided.

There were just a handful passengers at present in their coach. She didn't know that at night the trains too transformed not unlike those people who toil all day and then let loose at night. The few people who rode at this hour were different too. They were dreamers who dreamed of a better tomorrow. She thought this is how it should be in the daytime too, echoing the thoughts of every Indian.

She was surprised to see the coaches had no doors. The ceiling fans made a lot of noise just like the propellers of world war planes, and just like their old counterparts they too saw a war everyday arguably on a smaller scale. Every year more than a couple of thousands die on the rail tracks of Mumbai. If it goes like this at some point in the future these fans would have seen more deaths than the world war planes. But life and train continued unaffected, indifferent to joys and misery. The announcements were made in Hindi, English, and Marathi as the train started to roll.

The trains in Mumbai were a symbol of life, transient, flowing, never stopping.

Ninety Five

"LET'S SIT SOMEWHERE?" Lucia suggested as the train picked pace.

"You wanna stand here? Near the gate?" Kabir replied, as he leaned outward having grabbed the safety stanchion. The wind blew his hair back, and for a second his face was transformed.

"Okay..." Lucia walked towards Kabir and stood on one side taking support of the grab rail, a safe distance away from the entrance.

"I was just thinking about Spain and how kids travel in train and if there were no doors there too... it's dangerous to..." Lucia didn't complete the sentence as she looked at the world zipping past her at speed and to look down was to see it go faster. She didn't have to say anything further as her expression conveyed more than any words could. Her hands made sure that her grip was tight while Kabir looked on a bit amused yet empathetic. He explained to her there were doors, but they were just kept open all the time. How could he explain the dangerous circumstances people and even children had to navigate in this country as a matter of course.

Kabir loved to stand on the doorway, he liked the wind in his hair, and it gave him a sense of freedom. He would just stare out and forget everything else, all the worries, the stresses of life, would be simply blown off. Almost as if the wind were going right through the mind and clearing it up. Perhaps that's why a lot of men and even women could be seen standing on the doorway looking out. Most of them can be seen holding an intense, strong expression on their faces. Standing at the doorway with the trains going at 100 kmph was risky but people loved doing that. It also helped in the heat, but the bigger reason was that it gave them strength to face the challenges of living in a city like Mumbai. Earning money was not difficult here but everyone was chasing a dream. And if luck were on your side then you wouldn't be chasing it alone.

Ninety Six

"DO PEOPLE STAND like all the time?"

"Yeah. And I love it too. I like the wind in my hair."

Kabir stood almost leaning out of the doorway while Lucia remained a little further inside, holding the grab rails tight. As the train sped forward so did their thoughts.

"Do you wanna try standing this side?" asked Kabir.

"Yeah, okay, sure."

Lucia let go of the grab rail and held onto the stanchion in the centre and could feel the wind blowing over her. It was thrilling. Kabir had come to stand opposite her. She felt safe in his company and smiled at him through her big eye lashes. His hands were holding onto the grab rails behind him. He would lean forward and then his hands pulled him back.

The fleeting nature of their encounter rocked them forward and back.

"I feel a little unsure about this..."

"Feels good, nah..."

"Now I can understand why people like to stand here..."

"Hey, tell me something. What colours would you use to paint me?" Kabir stepped a bit closer.

"I like that question..."

Lucia's imagination had started to paint. She stood holding onto the pole in the centre with both her arms and was resting her head against it dreamily and gently swaying with the motion of the train. Her little wisps of hair flew gently into her face.

"Warm colours..." she said.

"What are warm colours?" Kabir used one hand to delicately move those hair aside from her face, sliding them back behind her ears. The slightest of the touches felt electrifying, sending currents through every little cell in Lucia's body.

"Warm colours... Means orange... Yellow... Red..." Lucia spoke unaware, pausing at every word. Deliberation was not a choice but an effect. Her eyes had met Kabir's, and she couldn't look away. Kabir gazed at her in rapture as if nothing else existed. But who was under whose spell it couldn't be said. They were both under the spell of love.

The words they spoke next were whispers... a rhythm... a movement... Perhaps they were not words but a disguise of love...

Rumi said it was love until the union. The train, the thoughts, the beating of the heart all finally synced to the sounds of the *damru*.

Shiva danced.

Ninety Seven

"YOU ARE VERY pretty..." he breathed.

"And you are an amazing human being..." Lucia said with a sigh.

"Thank you... I'll take that. I thought you would call me handsome!" Kabir grinned.

"Oh come on... I just met you today!"

"I noticed you had a tri-colour thing going on today..."

"I tried to carry India with me."

"Good plan."

"Yeah."

"They say if you come to India once, you always come again..."

"Who says that?"

"They."

"Hahaha... Okay."

"They are the people you never meet."

"Yeah... who knows... I think India still has a lot to offer me. Including a lot of stories."

"I think a lot of people here would like to learn ballet. And I doubt there are many ballet teachers here..."

"I don't think there are any...?"
"Buenos dias..."
"Very good... Muy bien!"
"I also know... Un... Dos... Tres..."
"Fantastic... And Catalan...? You know Catalan?"
"Nope!"
"It's okay... I'll teach you..."
"...."

The words exchanged didn't matter, they were all words of love. In that moment they were drunk and not on alcohol. He was singing, she was in ecstasy.

Ninety Eight

THE TRAIN CAME to a stop and Kabir pulled Lucia towards him by her arm. It was the touch of a lover.

They got down the train hand in hand, heart in heart. Sometimes all it takes is a stranger to know the thirst, sometime all it takes is a moment to quench it, sometimes… They both had bared themselves, seen the typhoons in the other and with a gentle stroke of compassion calmed them. What closeness is in the meeting of spirits is what they call love.

"I'm all smiles," Lucia grinned, her eyes like twin stars.

"I've have that effect on people!" Kabir winked at Lucia.

Lucia had her flight in a few hours, and she would be back to her city and her work. Kabir would go back to his city and join the job he had applied for. But tonight they were with each other. Tonight it didn't matter what would happen in the future. Tonight it just mattered that there was someone's hand each had to hold onto. Maybe this day will become a memory that will bring a smile on their faces when they are alone. Maybe the memory would fade away as they go back into the grind of the daily life. Maybe they will remember it again when they are alone.. Maybe... who is to say what the future will be.

Like when at 3 in the morning Simi, who hated to be disturbed in her sleep, was woken up by a phone call and had the choicest of words ready for the caller on the tip of her tongue but unfortunately she just couldn't use them. It was because she heard Kabir's voice at the other end.

"Hi Simi... Yaar, I had come to pick the bag..."

"*What yaar...you don't even let me sleep...*" Simi grumbled. It would take her more than a couple of minutes to drag herself out the bed. She didn't want to awaken her family as she carefully bolted the door behind her, dragging the heavy bag and went out.

Ninety Nine

LUCIA RESTED HER head against the windowpane of their cab, the motion was bringing in an inertia of sleep. Walking so much in a day had something to do with it. She still had to go the airport and then catch the flight. And then another flight from Delhi. It seemed a tedious task as she thought about what lay ahead, flight to Delhi... change flight to catch the long flight to Barcelona, and then the drive to her home before she could finally hit the bed. But her mum would say eat before you sleep. And she wondered whether she would even be able to sleep or would she be too excited.

Meanwhile, a certain Kabir sat making faces looking in the rear view mirror.

"I think my face looks fatter after drinking." A considered opinion of a contented soul.

Lucia laughed shaking her head that shook off some of the inertia, and Kabir laughed along. He was hitting the right chords.

"You know, I read in a magazine that women like men with a sense of humour, 66% more..."

"Okay..." Lucia turned her eyes. Her head still resting against the windowpane, but he had her attention now.

"You know what that means?"

"What?"

"That you should give me your phone number."

"It was written in the magazine as well, hmm."

"Yeah... it was also written that don't tell, you read all this in the magazine."

The sleep was driven back from her eyes as she laughed. Kabir shifted a little closer to her. With a sudden burst of energy Kabir turned around facing Lucia putting his arm behind on the seat.

"I don't know about the rest of your month in India, but I hope this one day washed all of the bad experiences away."

Lucia shifted herself and adjusted her body towards Kabir, looking into his eyes. They were so clear she thought.

"It was a good day."

"Because it's a good country..."

"It is..."

"I mean, it can get better... I love this country and I can't go out of here... You know... I mean I can travel to other places. But I gotta live here..."

"That's good."

Lucia was amused as she heard Kabir talk. He was reeling under the slight effects of alcohol that was giving the gentle nudges to make Kabir sway like a hot air balloon.

"And your friend Carla works here..."

"Yeah, she does... She is a sweet girl."

"And you completely ignored me when Carla was present!"

"No, that's not true!"

"You did, and I was jealous of her."

"No... Don't be!"

"Well, I am... And she has your phone number as well."

"You don't know that?"

"Does she?"

"Yeah, she does." Lucia admitted.

"Simi is bringing the bag, she was sleeping. She thought we would go back to her in the evening."

"Oh, we must have disturbed her. She is a sweet person."

"Yeah, she is. But she is just a friend."

"Yeah, I could see that." Lucia hid her amusement at this extra clarification that Kabir offered.

"Are you jealous of her?"

"Do you want me to say yes?"

"Well, you should, she has my phone number as well!" Kabir quipped.

He got out of the car with surprising dexterity as he saw a figure coming out of the gate. A visibly annoyed and sleepy Simi. Kabir got the bag and kept it in the boot of the cab.

Lucia got down and hugged Simi (who got surprisingly alert at this hug) and apologized for disturbing her sleep. Simi invited her up for food even in her sleep, as was her wont.

Hundred

ONCE EN ROUTE, Lucia called her mother to inform her that she was heading to the airport to board her flight.

"You wanna say hi to her?" And before Kabir could protest or prepare himself, Lucia handed the phone to Kabir making him fumble nervously. Lucia's mother had as much understanding of English as Kabir had of Spanish. Kabir was completely taken aback by this gesture and Lucia thoroughly amused. She was excited to meet her mother and she just couldn't wait to be with her and see her reaction at all the colourful gifts she had bought for her.

At the airport, Kabir brought out her luggage and helped her with the bag. She was not clumsy like him and in a quick snatch, jerk, and twist, had the bag around and mounted on her back. Kabir wanted to say something, but words wouldn't come, and he went over to the screen to look at the flights departure board. Lucia came from behind and held his hand.

They hugged each other in a tight embrace, and she spoke several words in Spanish that his brain couldn't interpret but his heart understood. It was difficult for both of them to let go, but then it happened almost instantly, like how the birds learn to fly, like how a toddler learns to walk. There were several emotions waiting to be expressed that only silence could convey.

Lucia looked back at Kabir as she passed through security. She kept turning back after every few seconds and every time she found him there standing with a smile. She was soon inside and yet Kabir still standing there. He looked forlorn as his eyes couldn't see her drifting in the crowd. But then she showed up one last time and flew him a kiss that landed as a smile on his lips. Lucia went off to collect her boarding pass and the formalities in the airport got her busy. She would swim in the same thoughts that Kabir was floating in right now. Later, when Kabir would have drifted into sleep, those thoughts would put her to sleep too as they both dreamt, they would meet each other in a hazy shade of reality.

Kabir stood there not knowing what to do with Lucia out of sight. He stood his ground for a while, absentmindedly though. Not knowing what to do next, he was loitering around the shops and stalls at the airport. He saw people sitting and waiting to receive people or people who had been dropped off. Motivated by an excited heart and lingering thoughts, he chose to sit down for a cup of tea before he finally made his way out of the airport.

The first rays of the dawn were still en route, yet to jump up over the horizon and Kabir was sleepy as a child who had been on a long journey away from home. He would have liked a few hours' sleep as quite suddenly he felt all the walking done in the day climb up through his feet, turning into a big yawn as it reached his face. He was so full of sleep that it was leaking out as tears. He didn't even have the strength to go home.

Kabir found a park nearby and a friendly enough bench and didn't realize when sleep had him cradled in its arms.

Epilogue

HE WOKE UP with his phone vibrating in his pocket and the Sun high up in the sky. Sounds of the day pervaded his ears along with wakefulness in his body. The time was well past 11 and he had missed his train home. And now he had missed the call.

A loud noise made him look up to see an airplane soar over him in the sky. He was reminded of the video Lucia had made for him. She must be way past Indian borders by now, he thought as he played the video. It was a short one and in it she mentioned her phone number...

He tried calling the number, but as expected, it was switched off, with Lucia in her flight. And then, still sleepy, he called back the missed call on his mobile.

"Hello?"

"Is that Kabir Singh?"

"Yes, speaking?"

"Hi, we wanted to talk about your song. We want to use it in our film. Can you meet?"

"Which song...?"

"Que sera sera..."

As he disconnected the call after the rather long conversation, tumultuous thoughts swirled in his mind. It was a major production house and they wanted to use one of his songs. He had agreed to it, still wondering if all this was a dream as he kept staring at his phone.

SHE WAS WOKEN up by the flight attendant who had come to serve the in-flight lunch. She had had the strangest dream. It was a beautiful one, and even though she couldn't remember it, she was smiling. She looked out the window, a vast endless desert was visible far beneath. They were flying above the Sahara, she guessed or perhaps over central Asia somewhere. She straightened herself in the seat and unfolded the tray as the flight attendant placed the platter. Her mouth was dry. She had some water and ate her lunch and drifted back to her unfinished dream.

A couple of hours later she woke up to the sound of the Captain announcing their landing.

As she looked out at the setting sun, she played the video Kabir had made again. She closed her eyes listening to his voice.

Que Sera Sera...

> *I'm watching my worries end...*
> *I'm witnessing it myself...*
> *What is, is all I see...*
> *All I see is you and me...*
> *Que sera sera...*

* * *

Author Bio

Sohrab Khandelwal is a storyteller and has been indulging the flights of imagination ever since a child. *Que Sera Sera* is his debut book and has been adapted into a film with him as a director. The film has won BAFTA Qualification.

He started as a stage actor at the age of 10. Always on the move since his father was in a transferable job, he studied in 16 different schools that allowed him to interact with many people. In 2006, he started his theatre production in Chandigarh while pursuing a Bachelor degree in Computer Science Engineering.

He continued to act, write and direct several plays and completed his degree. He took up a job with an IT giant, Infosys, in Pune, balanced his job and theatre and completed a course in scriptwriting. Finally, in 2013, he quit his job and moved to Mumbai, where he started working as a full-time actor.

www.sohrabkhandelwal.com

Connect with the author:
www.Instagram.com/sohrabkhandelwal/
www.Twitter.com/sohrabsunny/
www.facebook.com/sohrabkhandelwal/
www.linkedin.com/sohrabkhandelwal/